**JON STEINER** grew up in Washington, D.C. He has lived in Australia since 2000. He studied creative writing at the University of Technology, Sydney. This is his first book. He lives in Tempe with his wife and kid.

JONSTEINER.NET

Spineless Wonders
ABN 98156041888
PO Box 220
Strawberry Hills
New South Wales
Australia 2012
www.shortaustralianstories.com.au

First published by Spineless Wonders 2015

Text © Jon Steiner
Edited by Josh Mei-Ling Dubrau.
Copyediting by Bronwyn Mehan

Illustrations, cover and typesetting by Zoë Sadokierski

All rights reserved. Without limiting the rights under copyright reserved above, no part of this publication may be produced, stored in or introduced into a retrieval sysem, or transmitted, in any form or by any means (electronic, mechanical, photocopying, recording or otherwise) without the prior written permission of the publisher of this book.

Typeset in Adobe Garamond Pro 11pt
Printed and bound by Lightning Source Australia

National Library of Australia Cataloguing-in-Publication entry
The Last Wilkie's and other stories/Steiner, Jon
1st ed.
ISBN: 978-1-925052-16-9 (pbk)
ISBN: 978-1-925052-17-6 (ebk)

A823.4

**B.K.,**
FÜR DICH

# THE LAST WILKIE'S

AND OTHER STORIES

BY

**JON STEINER**

with illustrations by
ZOE SADOKIERSKI

# CONTENTS

| | |
|---|---|
| **01** | ROBBER |
| **06** | SCREWS |
| **08** | UNPACKING |
| **12** | TURTLES |
| **14** | SATURDAY |
| **18** | A FACT |
| **22** | SANTO NINO |
| **26** | TWINKLE |
| **28** | BEATA |
| **31** | GAIL |
| **32** | JUNGLE TRAIN |
| **47** | LIEBESTOD |
| **48** | OPEN FOR INSPECTION |
| **54** | HOW TO INSTALL |
| **56** | FLEAS |
| **62** | RIGHTS OF MAN |
| **64** | POIOUMENON |
| **73** | TOOTH |

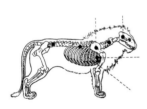

| | |
|---|---|
| **74** | CONTRACT |
| **81** | MORNING MEETING |
| **85** | SYMPTOMS |
| **90** | NORTHWEST PASSAGE |
| **92** | BUILDING |
| **95** | BOWLING |
| **97** | SUMMIT |
| **106** | 4 goths at the late nite petrol station window |
| **108** | EXPOSURE |
| **115** | INSTRUCTIONS |
| **116** | NOVEL |
| **121** | THE |
| **122** | GECKO |
| **129** | SHADY OAKS |
| **136** | THE LAST WILKIE'S |
| **160** | Acknowledgements |
| **162** | Notes |

# ROBBER

**THE CONVERSATION HAD STALLED,** so when the CD finished playing there was an awkward silence. Eric cleared his throat and said, 'Jamie, man, it's really great to see you.' He reclined on the couch, the still-smoking bong perched on his belly, his sandalled feet splayed across the coffee table. 'Seriously. We don't see you enough. You gotta come over more often.'

Jamie leaned forward on his chair and rested his elbows on his knees. 'Yeah, totally, man, it's so fucking great to see you guys, you know?' He looked from Eric to Ann and back again, nodding earnestly. Ann blinked several times and chewed on her thumbnail.

'I should put on more music,' said Eric, and commenced the involved process of getting up. 'What do you guys feel like listening to?'

'Some, like, jazz, maybe?' said Jamie.

'Yeah, sure, that can be arranged,' said Eric, and left the room.

Jamie turned to Ann. 'You've been pretty quiet over there in that armchair,' he said. 'How you doing?'

'Um, okay,' said Ann. 'Sorry, I'm just stoned I guess.'

He grinned and nodded. 'Yeah, huh? Totally.'

Some minutes passed. Jamie tapped out a little rhythm on the coffee table with his index fingers, and then closely examined his pack of cigarettes. Ann coughed quietly and cleared her throat, then shifted a bit in her chair and looked at the floor. There then commenced the tinkling of a piano, joined presently by a trumpet and drum kit, and Eric returned to resume his supine position on the couch. 'It's weird, man,' he said as he settled himself back down.

'What?' said Jamie.

'I got totally spooked when I was in there looking through the CDs. There was some freaky noise just outside the window and I totally thought someone was lurking out there, casing the house. A robber.'

'A robber!'

'Yeah, or something. My heart was in my throat. I was like literally frozen with fear for a moment.'

'So what was the noise really?'

'Well, I finally forced myself to go and look out the window, but I couldn't see anything. I'm sure I just hallucinated it or something. But it really sounded like crunching leaves underfoot and crinkling nylon windbreaker and the creak of a person's weight being supported by the windowsill and maybe a boot clunking against the side of the house as they hoisted themselves up to look in.'

'That's pretty fucking specific, man. You're kind of freaking me out now. Like what if there seriously is someone outside casing the house, and he sees three totally stoned wusses in here, easy prey, and fucking comes in and kills us?'

Ann hugged her knees to her chest and closed her eyes.

Eric said, 'No, come on, man, there's not. I don't mean to freak you out. I'm sure it was all in my head. The wind probably blew some leaves and maybe a branch fell from the tree out there. I'm just so stoned, I imagined all that other stuff.'

They sat quietly for a while, listening to the music. Then Jamie said, 'Wouldn't it be fucked up, though, if that really happened? Like, if some crazy guy just came bursting in, yelling and stuff?'

'Well, yeah it would be fucked up,' said Eric. 'I am so fucking stoned right now, I have no idea how I would react. I think I would just sit here and watch the guy, like he was in a movie or something. Completely detached. In a way, it would be kind of interesting just to see what it was like.'

'Yeah, it would. Hey, you could start like a service or whatever, where you can hire someone to go to stoned people's houses and pretend to be a robber so they can see what it's like to have that happen.'

'Hey, that is such a cool idea! You would be good at that.'

'Yeah? I would?'

'Yeah, you definitely would. I could totally see that. Hey you should do it, man! Do it right now for us!'

'Yeah? Seriously? You want me to pretend I'm a robber?'

'Yeah! Come in and be all scary and stuff.'

'Okay! I'll do it.' Jamie scurried off to the kitchen and they heard the back door slam.

'This is gonna be cool,' said Eric.

Ann smiled feebly.

Several minutes went by. 'What's he waiting for?' asked Eric. Then, 'Should I pack another bowl?' Ann nodded, so he did and they had some bong hits. Eric put the bong on the coffee table and tossed the lighter down beside it. Just then, there was a loud bang from the kitchen and Jamie stormed into the room holding a garbage bag in one hand and brandishing a long carving knife in the other.

'Alright, don't pull any shit or I will cut your fucking throats! I swear to god! I want everything of value. Everything of value in the house, I want it brought here, I want it in this bag. Right fucking now!'

Eric was enjoying it tremendously and grinning idiotically so Jamie dropped the garbage bag and backhanded him across the face. 'You think something is funny, motherfucker? I will show you funny. I'll wipe that fucking smile off your face! I will fucking kill you!'

Ann had started crying quietly, so Jamie now turned his attention to her. 'Stop your fucking crying, you skinny bitch!'

Eric's nose was bleeding. 'Jesus fucking Christ, Jamie! What the fuck is wrong with you?'

Jamie grabbed him by the shirt, pulled him up off the couch, and threw him onto the floor. 'Shut the fuck up!' He kicked Eric in the ribs several times. Then he picked up the garbage bag and went around the room, examining various articles. 'You got nothing here,' he said, scooping all the DVDs into his bag. 'You don't have jack shit. What about money? You got any fucking money at least?'

Eric was moaning. He clutched his side with one hand and held his bleeding nose with the other. 'You fucking psycho, Jamie! I think you broke my fucking ribs!'

Jamie crossed the room and stood over Eric. 'I told you to shut the fuck up.' He turned to Ann. 'And I told you to stop fucking crying.'

He grabbed Ann by her wrist, pulled her out of the armchair and threw her down onto the floor next to Eric. 'This your fucking girlfriend? Huh? This your skinny bitch?' He grabbed her collar and ripped her shirt off. She crossed her arms over her bare chest. 'She's got no tits!' yelled Jamie. 'Look at that. I got bigger tits than this bitch.' He bent down over Ann and tried to pull her arms open.

Eric lunged up off the floor and hit Jamie on the side of the head with the heavy glass ashtray. Jamie reeled backwards and went down, flattening the coffee table and landing hard against the television cabinet.

'What the fuck is wrong with you?' screamed Eric. 'It was supposed to be pretend! Only pretend!'

Jamie groaned and clutched his head. His legs jerked spasmodically and he rolled from side to side. Then he struggled to his feet. Blood was running down his face. He looked around in bewilderment for a moment and then ran out of the house.

'You okay?' said Eric to Ann. She shivered. Eric went to put his arms around her but she said, 'Don't.'

They just lay on the floor then, and listened to the jazz.

# SCREWS

HOWIE HAD A STRANGE COMPULSION: every morning he would get his Phillips head screwdriver out of the drawer in the kitchen and go around his house tightening screws. He would often proclaim his simple philosophy to his dog (who was the only person around to listen): 'Our world is entirely held together by screws. Big screws here, little screws there, and yet we take them completely for granted. If we are not diligent about keeping them all tightly intorted, our entire civilisation will quite literally crumble to the ground.'

There were four hundred and sixteen screws in Howie's house. It took him an hour and ten minutes each morning to go around and tighten them all, starting with the screws that held the doorknob on the front door and finishing with the screws that held the handle on the drawer where he kept the screwdriver.

After he was finished with the ritual, he would sit down at the kitchen table to read the paper. One fine morning, the wrought-iron light fixture on the kitchen ceiling (whose three screws he had overlooked the entire time he'd lived in that house) came loose and crashed down on Howie's head, crushing his skull all over the newspaper. In the ensuing excitement his dog stepped on some broken glass and got a pretty bad cut on his paw, which later became infected and the whole leg had to be amputated. The dog got used to having only three legs pretty fast though, and after a while he couldn't really remember ever having had four.

# UNPACKING

CHESTER WAS ON BART, headed for Oakland. The temp agency had gotten him three days of work there. He didn't really know anything about Oakland except that it would cost three dollars each way to take BART under the bay. So, six dollars a day to get to and from work. Which represented one hour of his pay. In other words, one-seventh of each workday would be spent just recouping what it cost him to be there.

Oakland, it turned out, was a pretty run-down city with a mostly black population. The job, it turned out, was unpacking components of workstations in a brand new office building. They had already been delivered to each office by other people, and would be assembled later on by other people still; all he and the other three temps had to do was unpack the components from their cardboard and plastic wrapping. Of the four temps, he was the only white guy. The others were all black. Of the other three, one guy was about his age and two were considerably older.

A white guy in a tie explained the work to them, which took about one minute. Then they set to work. They each had a box cutter. Slash the cardboard, rip it off. Pull the desktops, chairs, partitions and drawer units out of the plastic wrapping. Gather all the trash into giant garbage bags and leave them by the door.

They went through like a whirlwind, room after room, hardly speaking, working with a manic fury. Chester wasn't sure who, if anyone, was setting this pace, but he found it rather exhilarating and sensed that the other guys did too. They worked together like four components of a perfect machine. An unspoken thing developed between Chester and the other young guy: they were the clean-up boys. At the end of each room, while the two older guys had a rest, either he or the other young guy would pick up one of the giant garbage bags and hold it open, the other would nod, and then the two of them would sweep across the room together, the non-garbage bag holder shovelling the cardboard and plastic into the bag with both hands. In this way, each room was cleared in about a minute. They left the full garbage bags by the door, as instructed.

Around lunchtime, the white guy with the tie came and found them. 'Okay, how 'bout you all finish this room and then take an hour lunch break,' he said. They murmured their assent and the white guy departed. They worked their way through the room, and then the clean-up boys did their thing.

'Should we do the next room?' said one of the older guys, peering into it through the doorway.

The other young guy replied, 'Naw, that white man told us after this room we should take our lunch break,' and then immediately looked terribly embarrassed. 'Sorry,' he said to Chester, apologising for having said 'white'.

What Chester felt at that moment is hard to explain. One part of it was, *huh, so this is what it feels like to be the only person of a different race in a group*. Another part of it was, *no big deal, my friend, the guy is white, after all; it's a factual statement*. And yet another was, *Hey, look at me, I'm hanging out with black guys!* But there was something more, something Chester couldn't quite put his finger on. That event, being apologised to by the other young guy merely for having qualified the skin colour of the man who was their supervisor, it seemed important in some way. It was certainly very considerate of him. Would a white person apologise to a black person under the same circumstances? Maybe these guys did not interact with white people much and weren't quite sure how to be around him.

But really, the main thing was, Chester did not want to be associated with that white man with the tie. He was with his comrades right here in the trenches, unpacking office furniture. He felt far more of a kinship with them than he did with the supervisor. For him, skin colour wasn't the issue, it was social class: worker versus manager. Maybe he didn't like the skin colour being mentioned because it moved him against his will over to the boss side of the equation.

But then again, he was here having a drunken summer doing temp jobs and bumming around San Francisco, and if he ever was really broke or in trouble he could always call upon his parents for financial help, a luxury that it was quite unlikely any of his putative comrades had. And in a couple of months he would be returning to the east coast, back to his parentally-funded very expensive small liberal arts college to continue working on his Bachelor's degree, something his comrades did not and could never hope to have. Whatever he might wish in his idealistic liberal heart, he was far closer to the white man than to his co-workers.

They all went off their separate ways for lunch, then reconvened and resumed unpacking.

\*

Their frenetic pace ended up working against them. By the end of the second day they'd unpacked all the workstations and were told their services were not needed for a third day. One of the older guys, whose name was Ben, approached Chester and held out his hand.

'Hey, man. I just wanted to say it's been really great working with you.' Ben smiled. He was missing several teeth. 'I was thinking maybe we should get together sometime. Go to a bar, have a beer or something. Let me write down my phone number for you.'

Chester thanked him and gave some noncommittal response, politely took the piece of paper and filed it in his wallet. He found this very touching, but also weird and awkward. He knew he would never call Ben. They had hardly spoken to each other. None of them had spoken much throughout the two days. Maybe Ben was the sociable type, or was looking to make new friends. Maybe he was a Christian. Maybe he was just really lonely. But Chester's life in San Francisco was pizza slices, cheap malt liquor, bong hits, minimum-wage temp jobs, roaming the gritty streets in the middle of the night, riding around aimlessly on buses and streetcars on days when there was no work, having long existential discussions with homeless men on park benches, imagining that he was learning Important Things about life and the world, and waiting for it to be time to go back east, back to the idyllic bubble that was college.

Maybe if Chester had been older and wiser, he'd have given Ben a call, or at least considered it. Maybe he would eventually learn some Important Things. But not that summer in San Francisco. His heart was full of love for his brother, but he was still so young.

# TURTLES

**SHRIMPY LAUGHED HARD AND COUGHED.** 'What the fuck are you doing?!'

Elaine smiled up at him. 'Sitting in a cardboard box, what's it look like?'

'Okay,' he said and went into the kitchen.

'What's in all those bags?' she shouted to him.

'Cotton,' he yelled back, dumping it out onto the floor.

'Okay,' she answered.

Shrimpy found the glue and got to work. Soon the fridge was covered with cotton balls and drippy wet glue. He sat in a chair and drank iced tea and admired his work.

Elaine wandered in. 'What'd you do with all the magnets?' she asked. He pointed to the silverware drawer. Elaine tried out the fridge, opened and closed the door a few times. She ran her hand over the cotton and some of it came off.

'Still wet,' said Shrimpy.

'Yeah.'

'Did anyone call me?'

'Oh yeah. Mike did.'

'What'd he say?'

'He said to call him.'
'Is he at home?'
'I think so.'
'Hmm.'
'Maybe you should spray-paint the cotton different colours.'
'Hmm.'
'Where'd you get it?'
'Found it on the street.'
'Hmm.'
    Elaine went back into the living room and Shrimpy opened and closed the fridge a few more times.

# SATURDAY

**I WAKE UP AND IT'S SATURDAY** and the sun is in my face and I'm in Brooklyn. I get out of bed and walk out of my room and there are Lynne and Alex and I say good morning. They don't really answer. They seem to be having a fight. They go into their room and close the door and I stand alone and look out the window at the cars down on Flatbush Avenue and it's Saturday. I pet the dogs and walk into the kitchen and look in the fridge and sit on a chair.

I spent all week waiting for Saturday so I could do all the things I wanted to do and now it's finally Saturday and I have no idea. Also I have a hangover.

At the party last night, I drank wine, then beer, then gin, then whiskey, then more beer. I came home at 4 am.

I should do some laundry and write some emails and go grocery shopping. I want to write a great movie, take great photographs, play great music. I sit on a chair in the kitchen and drink some water and then I go in the bathroom and take a shit.

Jason is in his room with the door open, sprawled on his bed asleep, AM talk radio blaring. Lynne and Alex come back out of their room. Jason wakes up. It is decided that we are all going to the Delphi Coffee Shop at Hoyt and Livingston in downtown

Brooklyn for breakfast. We go and sit at the counter and eat and Jason seems sad and Lynne and Alex seem sad and an old woman next to me sends her toast back because it's not toasted enough and she talks to herself and Alex has to argue with the owner because we've been overcharged for our ham and cheese omelettes. We walk home along Atlantic Avenue and stop in at a junk store where a month earlier me and Alex saw some busted-up old tympani drums for sale. The price was a hundred and fifty bucks for each. Now the drums are in the back room and the price is forty bucks each and Alex haggles them down to forty bucks for two. Lynne and Jason leave to go back to the loft and me and Alex spend a long time examining all the drums to determine which ones could be fixed up. Eventually we select two but Alex doesn't have enough cash so we walk several blocks to the nearest cash machine where Alex withdraws his last forty bucks. Walking back from the bank I fall madly in love with a stunningly beautiful girl crossing Flatbush Avenue in the windy sunlight. I stare at her and she smiles sideways at me and my heart leaps and I almost run to her but then chicken out and hurry to catch up with Alex. As we turn the corner onto Atlantic Avenue I glance back one last time, but she has walked on.

We go back to the junk shop where Alex forks over the forty bucks and we each hoist a drum onto our shoulders and as we leave the store one old man comments to his companion, 'Must be a couple of kettle drummers.' We walk back home with the drums and when we get there the dogs jump up and down.

Alex rings his grandparents while Lynne does a crossword puzzle on her computer and Jason puts on his coat and goes somewhere and I wander around the house feeling vague and empty, beset by some grim dissatisfaction. What are the great things and who makes them and how are they made and what am I doing with my life and here I am in New York City and I may as well be anywhere because it's Saturday and I'm hung over and doing nothing and then Lynne goes out to take the dogs to Prospect Park and me and Alex get on our bikes and go for a ride around the neighbourhood. As we ride through Park Slope, Alex tells me that he and Lynne are probably going to break up and it's very sad and we ride down 9th Street and stop in front of Steve Buscemi's house. We stand there for a few minutes thinking, yep, there's Steve Buscemi's house, and then we ride home where we find Lynne standing outside with Noelle and a guy named Mark who's from London, and Lynne and Noelle and Mark go to get coffee at Coco's and me and Alex go inside and wait and forty-five minutes pass and Alex gets really anxious because he and Lynne are supposed to go to a dinner party at his boss's house and finally they get back and he and Lynne leave and I hang out with Noelle and Mark and the dogs are wrestling all over the apartment. This guy Mark from London is in a band so I talk to him about amps and Mark tells me his band practises on a pig farm outside London and then Jason comes home from wherever he was and we all laugh at a comic in the free weekly paper and then Noelle and Mark go home and I go and take another shit.

I wander around the apartment still with this wretched empty feeling. I sift through Jason's immense box of video tapes and find one labelled *Dangle Your Cat*, which is an indie movie that Jason edited and I haven't seen yet so I put it on and Jason comes into the living room, says, 'Hey, I know this movie,' sits down on the couch to watch it, and immediately falls asleep sitting up and snoring. I watch the whole movie and just as it ends Jason wakes up and puts on his coat and says he's going to a party and then to see the new *Star Wars* movie at midnight. I tell him I'm going to stay home and write a great movie. Jason says he looks forward to reading it when he gets home and then he leaves.

I sit on a chair at the window and watch all the people on the street below. I think of the beginning of that short film *Ambition* by Hal Hartley. *I want to be awed by my own accomplishments. I want to be compared to great men. I want to change people's minds, I want to set trends, destroy preconceptions. I want to be loved by beautiful women. I want my image of myself and my self to become one.*

I call a couple of people and leave messages and then I skulk around the house trying to think of a great movie idea or a great song and I plug in Alex's guitar and put on an Unwound CD and spend a while trying to learn some of the songs and an hour passes and Lynne and Alex come home from the dinner and I make myself a gin and water to take the edge off the hangover and smoke cigarettes in the hallway and Alex gets out his copper-coloured paint and starts painting his big canvas. Orrin comes downstairs from the fourth floor to borrow some glue and discusses the merits of taping sheets of plastic over the windows to lower heating bills and Lynne goes to bed and I go get some 22-ounce Country Clubs from Jorge's Grocery on the corner and then me and Alex sit down to drink them and watch the Jim Jarmusch film *Dead Man*.

*It is preferable not to travel with a dead man.*

Alex goes to bed and I stand at the window for a while staring down at the empty street and then finally go to my room and crawl into bed. Another Saturday has passed me by with nothing to show for it. How many more Saturdays have I got left before I die?

Couple thousand, at least.

Right?

And Sundays, as well.

So maybe there's still time.

# A FACT

'IT IS A FACT,' SHE SAID. 'The number of atoms in the universe is finite. It's an extremely large number – extremely large to our minds, at least – but still, a finite number. And each atom's position at any given moment could be described. Everything about it could be described. What type of atom it is, its location, direction, mass ... other stuff, I dunno.'

'Yuh,' he said.

'Also, all atoms have always existed. Always.' She picked his hand up off the table and planted her index finger in his palm. 'One of these atoms that makes up this skin cell here, it may once have been a dinosaur's toenail, and later it may have been a whale's optic nerve, and still later it may have been, I dunno, part of Beethoven's hair. And now it's part of you. All these atoms that make up *you* are billions of years old.'

'Hoo.' He examined his hand closely to see if there was any evidence of this.

'I could log the exact type and location of the seven octillion atoms that comprise your entire being, and keep track of them all as they move. If I had a really fast computer or whatever.'

'Hem.'

'I mean, it's always thought of – the world I mean – is always thought of as this chaotic place. Your cat gets hit by a car, your retirement fund gets wiped out in a stock market crash, there are floods in Bangladesh and droughts in Somalia, but it's all just a question of the positions and types of atoms. It's like weather. If you have enough data, you can make a prediction. Get me?'

'Yeah, yeah, I see what you're saying…'

'Okay, then think about this. A dead leaf is hanging from a tree branch. Brown and curled up. Then there comes a moment when it falls to the ground. At that moment, it's just a question of one atom. Cell walls deteriorate and molecules change, bonds between atoms break and form elsewhere, and then one final atom lets go and the balance of the leaf's attachment to the branch versus its weight shifts and it falls to the ground. Maybe a gust of wind hastens the process, but still – there is a point at which one atom more would have made the difference and kept that leaf on the branch a while longer. One atom!'

'Huh. Pretty crazy.'

'Well it sure makes you think.'

'That it does.'

'Yup.'

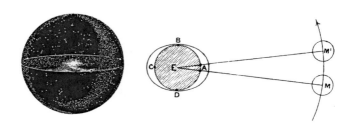

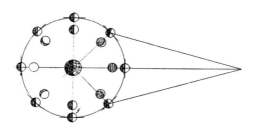

# SANTO NINO

**ONE AFTER ANOTHER,** the Cebuanos climb onto the wooden platform and kneel before the makeshift altar. With a silver ladle, Padre Valderrama anoints them with holy water, intoning the blessing each time in his nasal voice: *En nombre de Padre, de Hijo y de espiritu santo.* As they step down off the stage and back onto the sand, they rub their wet hair and grin.

Watching the proceedings from the banquet table, Magellan smiles with satisfaction. 'What a day, huh?' he says to the stocky, shirtless man beside him. 'How's it feel to be a Catholic, Humabon?'

'Feels great!' says Humabon, throwing a pork bone onto the pile and wiping his mouth with a silk cloth. 'Thanks again for teaching us about God and Jesus and stuff.'

Across the table, Humabon's wife, Humamay, cradles a small wooden statue of young Jesus dressed in an ornate velvet robe and wearing a gold biretta. 'This thing is so cool,' she says.

Magellan leans forward. 'Made in Flanders,' he tells her. 'Top quality.'

'Wow,' she says.

A gentle zephyr rustles the palms overhead, carrying upon it faint moans of pleasure from a nearby grass hut. All the men around the table – European and Cebuano both – exchange knowing smiles. Magellan cocks an enquiring eyebrow at Barbosa.

'Pigafetta,' explains Barbosa.

Serrão smiles and shakes his head. 'Such a pussy hound.'

'He calls it research,' says Barbosa.

'Yeah,' snorts Magellan, *'research.'*

They contentedly watch the baptisms for a while. Then, a few seats down the table, Datu Zula clears his throat. 'Too bad about Lapu-Lapu though,' he says.

The smile drains from Magellan's face and he turns slowly to glare at Datu Zula. 'Well, we tried with that guy, didn't we?' he says icily. He waves his goblet at his slave Enrique, who pushes himself off the palm tree he's been resting against and lopes over to the table to pour wine. 'Would have been great to have him and his people here today,' Magellan goes on, 'but I believe his exact words were, *Get the fuck off my island.*'

'*His* island!' snorts Humabon. 'I *gave* him that fucking island!' He slaps at a fly. 'I'm just too trusting of people, that's *my* problem.'

Serrão has been playing footsie under the table with Humamay, but now looks up sharply. 'Yeah, I still don't get why you gave a whole island to some guy you barely knew,' he says.

Humabon shrugs. 'He seemed alright at the time,' he says. 'I just wanted them to farm it and sell stuff at our market. Help boost our rep as a big trading centre.'

'Which worked brilliantly,' adds Humamay, 'until Lapu-Lapu started raiding the ships that came to trade. Now no-one comes.'

'What a dick,' says Barbosa.

'That's fucked up,' says Serrão.

'That's piracy,' says Magellan darkly.

The baptisms have finished and Padre Valderrama is packing

up his things. A group of the new Christians kneels before the massive wooden cross beside the stage, awkwardly practising their devotions.

Datu Zula clears his throat. 'Well, I've been thinking. Maybe we should just … you know…' He slowly runs a finger across his tattooed neck, leaving a smear of pig fat.

Barbosa shakes his head. 'Sorry, buddy. We have strict orders not to get involved in local politics.'

'Shit, man, I'll do it myself,' says Datu Zula. 'Just give me a couple of your gun boats for backup.'

'Not going to happen,' says Barbosa. 'Those orders come straight from the King and Queen of Spain.'

'This is part of it,' says Magellan quietly, almost to himself.

'Part of what?' asks Barbosa.

'The divine hand at work,' says Magellan.

'Divine hand?' says Serrão.

'God's grand plan for me,' says Magellan.

Barbosa, Serrão and de Soto exchange worried looks.

'Here we go again,' mutters de Soto.

Magellan fixes his gaze on the hills in the distance. 'Throughout this voyage, I have felt the hand of God guiding and protecting me. Many times I should have perished, but through His grace I have survived mutiny, disease and starvation. Thus have I come to understand that He has a divine plan, and I am His servant. God's will is that I should spread His word to the far corners of the Earth, bringing Christianity and civilisation to the savages. No offence,' he adds quickly to Humabon, who purses his lips, shakes his head and waves dismissively.

'Yes, okay,' says Barbosa cautiously, 'but what's that got to do with killing Lapu-Lapu?'

'I'm not talking about *killing* Lapu-Lapu,' says Magellan. 'I'm talking about *converting* him. No good Christian would commit piracy. So, problem solved.'

Everyone absorbs this information for a minute. Datu Zula looks disappointed. 'Well, but what if he still refuses to convert?'

'Then we kill him.'

Datu Zula claps. 'I love it!' he says.

Humabon smiles and nods.

Barbosa, de Soto and Serrão look at each other in dismay.

'I'm going to get Gomez to take me back out to the *Trinidad*,' calls the Padre to no-one in particular, heading down towards the boats.

Leaning against his tree, Enrique yawns.

Magellan swirls wine around in his cup, lost in thought.

Humamay holds up the Jesus statue. 'Hey, do you guys have any more of these?'

# TWINKLE

**TWINKLE Q. PERIWINKLE LIKED** those stories where someone was lost and adrift in the big wide scary world, but then by sheer luck and happenstance – or, perhaps, the hand of Fate – found something that gave their life meaning and set them on the right course. She was always on the lookout for that Thing for herself. But many years had gone by and the Thing had not yet presented itself to her.

Perhaps it's not a passive process, she thought one day. Maybe you just need to pick a thing and make it your Thing. She leafed through the newspaper and decided to pick her Thing at random from there, trusting destiny to be her guide. She closed her eyes, stabbed her finger onto the paper, then opened her eyes.

It was an ad for a large chain of hardware stores that said, 'All mowers 50% off!' Okay, then. That would henceforth be her Thing. Her guiding principle. The words by which she would live.

She cut out the ad and taped it to her bedroom wall, next to the mirror. Every night before she went to sleep, she looked at it and repeated the words ten times. Every morning when she woke up, she looked at it and repeated the words ten times. 'All mowers 50% off!' Whenever she was faced with adversity, she recited that phrase in her head. She thought constantly about how she could apply it to her life. She meditated on it daily.

But after a couple of years, it became apparent that the Thing she'd picked was a dud. I mean, all mowers 50% off? What the hell?

The next day, Twinkle bought an oboe and enrolled in an Italian language course.

# BEATA

**HAVE YOU BEEN TAKING DRUGS?**
*No*, mother, says Beata.
I know something is wrong. Mother's instinct.
I'm fine, alright? I'm actually really fine.
Go tell your father five minutes. And can you put the potatoes on the table.
Beata's father is in the garden, tying his beans to the trellis. Mum says five minutes, Dad!
Right-o, he calls back without looking up, be in in ten then.
Fifteen minutes later, Beata and her father are sitting at the table with Aunt Rosie.
Just a couple more minutes, guys, calls her mother from the kitchen. The gravy's not reducing.
Rosie is updating her Facebook status on her phone. Beata can see the telltale shade of blue reflecting off her glasses.
What are you putting as your status? she asks.
Rosie reads it back. 'Hungry and Christmas dinner is late as always.'
Seriously? says Beata, laughing. She'll see that and flip out!
Only joking, says Rosie. Just a general merry Christmas message. Nice to be with the family, isn't it?

Beata's father keeps peering over his shoulder, his mind still on the beans.

A turkey on a tray bursts through the doorway, followed by her mother. It takes its place in the centre of the table.

Looks lovely, says Rosie.

Beata's father picks up the carving knife. Thigh for you, Rosie? he asks.

Thanks, says Rosie, and holds out her plate.

Don't drip on the tablecloth! says her mother, and disappears back into the kitchen for the gravy.

Breast, Beata?

Uh, yeah, thanks, she says, thinking of her newly-pierced nipple. She kind of wants to show it to the family. Would that be weird? But if so, why exactly? They're family, and it's only a nipple. But also, would her motive be to share it with them, or to shock them? Or just to demonstrate that she is no longer the sweet, docile, compliant Beata that they have always known. This is the new, daring Beata now. Tough. Spontaneous. Free-spirited.

Isn't it?

Perhaps some fortification is required.

Shall I open the wine? she asks.

Good idea, says her father, plonking some white meat onto her plate. Beata reaches for the bottle and cracks the top.

Her mother settles into her chair with much sighing and hand wringing. I think I've overcooked the turkey.

It looks fine, says her father.

It looks wonderful, says Rosie.

Ronald, you're butchering that bird. Who wants potatoes?

What's the time? asks Rosie.

Half past, says Beata's mother, why?

We're supposed to Skype with Neville and Ange right now.

But we've only just sat down!

I thought dinner was going to be at five.

Well they can wait, I'm sure, can't they?

I'll send Neville a text, says Rosie.

Is there salad? asks Beata's father.

Yes, darling, it's in the kitchen, says her mother.

Ah.

Shall I just go and fetch it then, shall I?

Well, I thought we might want some. He looks around the table with an *oh-the-things-we-must-put-up-with expression.*

Beata's mother rises and stomps to the kitchen, returning shortly with the salad bowl, which she deposits heavily on the table next to him. He tosses it a bit and serves himself, then hands the bowl to Rosie. Her phone dings and she looks at it.

Neville says they're watching a movie and I can just text him whenever we're ready.

I've got a lovely Christmas pudding for afters, says Beata's mother. We can have it with coffee while we sing carols.

Oh, God, exclaims Beata, can we not do carols this year?

What? Her mother is shocked. You always love carols! I had the piano tuned especially for today!

I don't love carols anymore, Mum. That was when I was a kid.

What's wrong with carols? Everyone loves carols!

Not everyone loves carols!

You're on drugs, aren't you?

I am not on drugs!

Her mother stares at her hard. There's something going on with you, she says. What is it?

Beata sighs. Listen. I have something to show you guys. She starts to unbutton her shirt.

# GAIL

**THE PRINTER WAS NOT WORKING.** Gail checked the paper and pushed the green button a few times. 'Fuck.' She went back to her desk and clicked 'print' again. As she returned to the printer, it came to life and two pages emerged, warm and trembling. It reminded Gail of an insect giving birth. But don't insects lay eggs? thought Gail.

She went to Mark's office. It was empty. She left the two pages on his chair and went back to her desk.

# JUNGLE TRAIN

DISCREETLY – BECAUSE SHE KNOWS Malaysia isn't exactly a gay-friendly country, and knows that Michelle is super paranoid about it – Róisín slides her hand over and rests it on Michelle's leg. She waits for a response: a little hand squeeze, a sideways smile, an elbow nudge, anything. But Michelle doesn't acknowledge the hand in any way. She just continues reading her book. After a minute, feeling stupid, Róisín takes her hand away.

Across the aisle, Michelle's dad has been talking non-stop to her mum – or *at* her mum, to be more precise – about everything from the geology of the region to the socio-economics of rural subsistence farming in Southeast Asia to the various civil works projects he's observed out the window. He's also commented on every aspect of the Malaysian railway network, and of the train itself, which has turned out to be considerably more rustic than Róisín was expecting. Had she known that this thirteen-hour trip across the country was going to be in an ancient two-carriage affair with no dining car, she might not have agreed so readily to undertake it.

Still, after being in cities for a week, it's good to get out and see the countryside. In the couple of hours since they left Gemas, the train has stopped at several tiny hamlets, so small that there weren't even train stations; passengers just climbed aboard from the grass along the side of the tracks, hoisting boxes, baskets and bags up with them. The scenery is spectacular: dense jungle, sweeping valleys, majestic waterfalls. There are several women in burqas on board. At one point, everyone in the carriage wrapped themselves in white shrouds, laid out small rugs sideways on their seats and did their prayers, bowing and rising, bowing and rising, which was quite a sight. Róisín has never been anywhere so exotic and foreign and it's all very exciting and she'd love to be sharing the experience with her girlfriend, except her girlfriend has gone all weird on her.

It started pretty much the moment they landed in Kuala Lumpur and met up with Glen and Lee-Ann at the hotel. Róisín has been with Michelle in the company of her parents several times before when they've gone to Canberra for a visit, and has observed the strange family dynamics and their effect on Michelle – the silently judging mother, the loquacious jocularity-masking-anxiety father, and Michelle's regression into sullen and non-communicative teenager-dom. And she has been present at scores of phone calls between Michelle and Lee-Ann (almost daily, in fact) where Michelle, the high-flying corporate executive who manages an entire department of some two hundred people – and, as Róisín has witnessed on a couple of occasions, can be a pretty scary boss – transforms into a child, putting on a pouty face and talking in a baby voice: 'Hi, Mama. I'm okay. I had a bit of a tummy ache this morning but I had some soup and I'm feeling a bit better…'

But this, now, is something entirely different. Róisín has never felt so shut out by Michelle. In Canberra, they always had a good debrief in bed at the end of the day, laughing about the crazy family and reaffirming their bond. In Malaysia, Michelle has been disappearing into herself. And over the past couple of days it has become pretty extreme – they've hardly spoken a word to each other. But then they haven't had any private time to talk anything out, even if Michelle had been willing to. From Malacca, they spent an entire day taking two buses to Gemas, then all four of them slept in a dorm-style room, woke up ridiculously early, and here they are on the train.

It had seemed like such a good idea when Glen had proposed it. 'Lee-Ann and I are planning on travelling around Malaysia for a few weeks after my trade talks in K.L. Why don't we fly the two of you over to join us?' To Róisín, it was a potent and timely symbol of her acceptance into the family, and a welcome progression to the next level for her relationship with Michelle. Now she wonders whether they will even still be together at the end of this trip. If only Michelle would make eye contact, give her some sign that she's still in there, that they're still *them*. But despite all the amazing scenery passing by outside the window, and the incredible experience of being here on this train, Michelle has barely looked up from her book. Who does that? Can she really be that uninterested? Róisín wonders if she really even knows this person.

The lack of a dining car is also a problem. The train left Gemas at seven, so they stumbled bleary-eyed out of bed straight onto it, without time for breakfast. Róisín would kill for a coffee, but at this point, anything edible would do.

The train slows and comes to a brake-screeching stop in a moderate-sized town, one that actually has a train station. On the platform, a woman is holding a basket with some sort of food in it. 'Breakfast is served!' cries Glen cheerfully, and hurries down the carriage and onto the platform. Róisín is thrilled at the prospect of food but terrified that the train will leave without him. How long does the train stop here for? Could be only a couple of minutes.

He doesn't have his passport or phone on him. What if the train leaves without him? How would they find him again? It would be a serious nightmare. Michelle is still absorbed in her book and, across the aisle, Lee-Ann is knitting. Neither of them seems concerned in the least.

Róisín has to twist around in her seat to be able to keep an eye on Glen down on the platform. He's taking ages. He seems to be having some trouble communicating with the woman; maybe he's trying to work out what she's selling, or how much it costs. Then he appears to be cracking jokes, which the woman obviously doesn't get since she doesn't speak English, and she doesn't really look like the joking type anyway. He fumbles with his money, still not entirely familiar with the colourful ringgit notes. Róisín clenches her fists.

A whistle blows and the conductor gets back on board. The stationmaster walks purposefully along the platform carrying a green flag, pushing through all the people milling about, shouting something. There is a lot of activity and departure seems imminent.

*Come on, Glen. For fuck's sake, get back on the train!*

She prepares to run up the aisle, shouting for the train to stop, that they've left someone behind. But Glen finally completes the transaction and hustles back to the train, hopping onto the first step just as it jerks and starts moving. He comes down the aisle of the carriage holding four paper sacks triumphantly in the air. 'Fried bananas!' he announces, distributing them to everyone. Róisín takes hers gratefully. He may have almost given her a heart attack, but he did manage to get food. It's not coffee, but it'll do.

'Looks like we picked the right carriage!' he says as he settles back into his seat next to Lee-Ann. 'I just noticed that the windows don't open on the other one! Bet it's hot in there!'

'Actually – Dad, do you want to trade seats?' says Michelle suddenly. 'I think the view on this side is more interesting, but I'm just reading my book.'

'Oh! Well. I don't mind,' says her father. 'We can switch if you like.'

Without a word to Róisín, Michelle gets up and stands in the aisle, swaying with the rocking of the train as her dad crosses over and settles himself in beside Róisín. Michelle sits down next her to mother and goes back to her book. Róisín can feel her face flush. What was that about?

'Some people just don't have their priorities straight,' jokes Glen. He's referring to choosing the book over the view, but then realises it could also mean something else. He gives Róisín a little pat on the arm and says quietly, 'Maybe she just needs a bit of time out.' So he's noticed that something is up. Well, of course he has. How could he not? It's been pretty obvious. But it's still a shock to get outside confirmation. Róisín's eyes well up with tears. She nods and looks out the window, trying to keep it together.

Glen points at a farm they're passing. 'Looks like they're putting in a secondary irrigation canal there,' he says. 'That's good planning. It'll make that whole higher section of land arable in a few years.'

He continues his running commentary on the world outside the window until finally Róisín can't take it anymore. She needs a break. 'Sorry, Glen, just going to the toilet,' she says, getting up and climbing over him. She stands in the aisle for a moment, looking down at Michelle, who now is resting her head on Lee-Ann's shoulder with her eyes closed. Lee-Ann is staring straight ahead at the back of the seat in front of her, her knitting lying idle in her lap.

Róisín makes her way to the end of the carriage where the toilet is. In the vestibule, two young men are hanging out the door of the train, smoking cigarettes and joking around with each other. It looks like great fun. She pauses, considers asking for a cigarette and joining them. Their glances flicker over her, registering her existence and nothing more, and they go back to their conversation. She is too shy to ask, anyway, and doesn't speak the language. And there are probably cultural mores about a woman speaking to men she doesn't know, and, for that matter, smoking cigarettes; she doesn't know what might be considered inappropriate, so she gives up on the idea.

The toilet is not the cleanest she's ever seen. Róisín is careful not to let any part of her body or clothes touch anything as she sways with the rocking of the train, hovering over the hole in the floor through which she can see down to the track bed, the sleepers whizzing past in a blur. When she emerges, wiping her hands on her jeans since there were no towels, the two men are gone. She goes to the open doorway and leans out into the jungle.

What a thrill! Trees whip by only a metre from her head. The wind tosses her hair wildly. As the train enters a curve, the locomotive and front carriage curl around into view, and the majesty and grace of the old train rattling through the jungle make her want to weep with happiness. She tightens her grip on the handrail and leans even further out. It's almost like flying. She enjoys the danger – if she let go, she'd tumble to certain death – but not too much danger: as long as her hands can hold her, she's safe. The train goes over a small ravine and she looks straight down to the rocky creek bed at the bottom, stifling an urge to shout with excitement.

She wants so badly to go and get Michelle, ask her to come share this amazing experience. The Michelle of a week ago would have. Wouldn't she? Róisín's not even sure anymore. And now? She might, grudgingly, if pressed, but then would probably just glare at

Róisín reproachfully for being immature.

She goes back to her seat. 'Everything okay?' asks Glen as she climbs over him. 'How's your ... uh ... you know? Are you feeling better today?' Róisín's had the runs for a couple of days, and of course her girlfriend's father knows all about it and is asking. Cause, you know, why not.

'Yeah, I'm fine,' she says. 'It was only a wee.'

'Ah. So how's the toilet on this train?' asks Glen.

'It's not the cleanest I've ever seen,' she says.

Glen leans across her and points out the window as another small farm goes past. 'Now this is interesting,' he says. 'I keep seeing these goats that look very similar to the Boer goats we've got back home, only of a slighter build...'

\*

The day wears on. Glen falls asleep. Across the aisle, Michelle is still asleep on Lee-Ann's shoulder. When Róisín looks across, Lee-Ann turns and their eyes meet. Lee-Ann smiles wanly and nods, then goes back to her knitting.

The scenery, though still beautiful, becomes familiar and tiresome. Róisín gets out a sketchpad and tries to draw, but the movement of the train makes her lines look palsied, so she thumbs half-heartedly through a magazine and wishes she had a book, like Michelle. The sack of fried bananas barely touched the sides and Róisín is starving. The Malaysians on the train came prepared with packed lunches; only the four Westerners assumed there'd be a dining car. The train makes numerous stops, but only in those small, station-less hamlets. She hopes for a proper town with a proper station, where there might be someone on the platform selling food.

In the early afternoon, the train pulls into just such a station. A snack man climbs on carrying a couple of boxes in his arms and some bags slung around his neck, laden with chips and lollies and drinks. Róisín watches intently, waiting for him to begin hawking his wares, but he first sets his boxes down in a corner of the carriage and begins unwrapping and unpacking everything, laying it out on display. Bags of strange pink puffy chips are lined up on a seat, then little bags of lollies. He has several six-packs of juice boxes, which he begins unwrapping and setting out. As he removes each crinkly plastic wrapper, he deftly pops it out the open window. Róisín watches in horror as the wrappers flutter off into the pristine jungle. He pulls a bunch of small paper sacks out of a large plastic bag and sets them up on the seat, then sends the plastic bag fluttering out into the jungle as well.

'Oh, my God,' whispers Róisín, her hands on her cheeks.

Glen has seen it too. 'Well, you know, when I was a kid, we thought nothing of tossing rubbish out the car window when we went on road trips. We just had no idea. Of course, that would be unthinkable now. I guess it takes a while for those sorts of notions to change in any society.'

Finished setting up, the snack man is open for business. The dad sitting in front of Róisín and Glen goes over and buys a bag of lollies for his son. As the boy unwraps each one, he pops the wrapper out the window. The dad says nothing. Róisín no longer wants anything to do with the snack man's snacks.

Michelle wakes up, then stands up and stretches. She places her book on her seat and heads off towards the end of the carriage.

'I'm going to stretch my legs a bit too,' says Róisín. She climbs over Glen and goes to the vestibule. The toilet is occupied. She leans out into the wind again, glancing at the toilet door every few seconds, waiting for Michelle to come out.

After a few minutes, the latch turns and Michelle emerges. She looks a bit startled when she sees Róisín. 'Hey,' she says, and starts to head back to her seat.

'Michelle!' calls Róisín.

Michelle stops and turns.

'Come here a second.'

Michelle comes back to the vestibule. 'What is it?' she asks.

'I just wanted to say hi,' says Róisín. 'Hey, you should try hanging out the door, it's amazing.'

Michelle pokes her head out for a brief look. 'Yeah, cool,' she says. She starts back for her seat again.

'Michelle?' says Róisín.

'Yeah?'

'Come here.'

'What is it?'

'Just come here, I want to touch you.' She reaches for Michelle's hand.

'Are you crazy? Do you know what country we're in? Do you want to get us stoned to death?'

'Jesus, I'm not asking to make out with you!'

Michelle sighs and rolls her eyes.

'Michelle, is something the matter?'

'What do you mean?'

'You just seem ... distant. I mean ... like ... are *we* okay? Have I done something to piss you off or something?'

Michelle glares at her. 'You know, your needy insecurity is really not one of your more attractive features,' she says, then stalks off.

\*

Róisín is ready to be off this train. She has no concept of where they are or how much further they have to go, but the seats are uncomfortable and it's hot and she would prefer to not use the toilet again if at all possible. She needs to be alone with Michelle, to talk to her, ask what the fuck is going on. Michelle was the one who was so keen for the four of them to go travelling together. So what is she so pissed off about now?

The train pulls into a large town and a group of about twenty schoolkids get on. They're all wearing Garfield backpacks and school uniforms, which for the girls includes head coverings. They stand in the aisle, chatting and laughing. At each of the next several stops, a succession of small hamlets, a few of the kids get off the train to be met by dads waiting on motorbikes. The kids hop on the backs and they zoom off into the jungle. Róisín leans her forehead on the window, watching them disappear, and wonders what their lives are like. They all look pretty happy.

*

Róisín falls asleep for a couple of hours. When she wakes up, it's starting to get dark. There is no electricity on the train, so it gets dark inside the train as well. Too dark for Michelle to read anymore. The Muslims on the train do their prayers again, now just silhouettes bowing and rising in the shadows. This time, instead of seeming exotic to Róisín, it seems kind of spooky.

The train pulls into a large station, and Róisín spots a man on the platform with a small cart, selling something to eat. Glen sees him too. 'I'm going to go get us some food,' he says.

'It's alright, Glen,' says Róisín. 'I'll go this time.'

She goes to the end of the carriage, descends to the platform and approaches the man. He's selling bundles of banana leaves with something inside them. 'What is it?' she asks. He says something she can't understand. She shrugs and says, 'Four, please,' holding up four fingers. He puts four bundles in a plastic bag and she forks over some ringgit notes, keeping an eye on the train for signs of impending departure.

Just as she takes the plastic bag, the conductor finishes chatting to the stationmaster, throws his cigarette to the ground and blows his whistle. He grabs the handrail and swings up onto the step. The stationmaster walks along the platform holding up his green flag. Róisín can dimly make out Lee-Ann's head through the window, engaged in conversation with someone, presumably Michelle. Is anyone keeping an eye out to make sure Róisín doesn't get left behind? Would they even notice if the train left without her? Would they care? Would they try to find her? Well, they'd have to, really. Her passport and all her belongings are on that train. She doesn't even know the name of this town.

All she wants is some sign from Michelle that she still gives a fuck. Is that so much to ask? Is that being insecure and needy? It doesn't seem all that unreasonable. The conductor is standing in the doorway of the carriage, glaring at Róisín. He knows she's supposed to be on the train. He nods at her curtly, irritated. Why is she just standing there? She ignores him, staring at the window framing Lee-Ann's head. The conductor shouts something to her, holds up his arm to show his wristwatch. He looks conflicted. She shakes her head at him, keeping her eyes fixed on the window, waiting for someone to look out and check on her.

She just wants to scare Michelle a little. If the train starts moving, Michelle will realise that Róisín's not back. She'll look around suddenly, worried. 'Wait!' she'll shout. She'll run to the conductor. 'Stop the train! My girlfriend isn't back yet!' Róisín can jump onto the steps at the end of the last carriage and make her way triumphantly up to the seats, to everyone's relief.

People on the platform are staring at her. The conductor shouts something angrily, shrugs, and gives a wave to the engineer. The train lurches and starts to move. Róisín knows she still has a good fifteen or twenty seconds to leap on. All she has to do is run a few steps, catch the last handrail and swing herself up. The train picks up speed. She can't see Lee-Ann anymore, the window has moved too far along now. The conductor is leaning out the door, receding into the distance as he looks back at her. Every muscle in her body is tensed, ready to spring. She triangulates the trajectory of the last handrail against the acceleration of the train.

As the end of the train reaches her, she takes a couple of steps towards it, but then stops. She has miscalculated. It has picked up too much speed. There is no way she can make it.

She watches the back of the train disappear into the darkness. When she can no longer see it, Róisín starts laughing. The people around her recoil as if from a mad person, except for one old woman in a black headscarf, who drags a red plastic chair over and guides Róisín into it.

The old woman walks off, shaking her head. Róisín looks around at all the people watching her. They're waiting to see what she will do next. She reaches into the bag and pulls out one of the bundles of banana leaves, unwraps it to find a clump of sticky rice with nuts and shredded coconut. She takes a bite. It's delicious.

Well, whatever else, at least she now has plenty to eat.

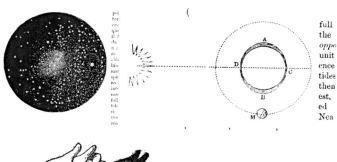

# LIEBESTOD

WELL, JASPER FINALLY got up the gumption to ask that Mabel from the feed store out to see the opry. He was admittedly a bit surprised when she said yes first and asked what was playing second. He told her *Tristan and Isolde*.

She said she preferred that Shostakovich.

Them Russkies is trouble, he told her. They got that Communism and all.

She rolled her eyes. They tore down that wall in 1990, she said, they don't got Communism no more.

Despite his better judgement, his ire rose. Well, Shostakovich didn't even write no oprys, he shouted.

She laughed that sweet laugh of hers, what never failed to melt his old heart. Course he did, she said and flicked her hair in that particular way. What about *Lady Macbeth*?

That were Verdi, he told her, getting madder 'n a dang polecat caught in a seed bag.

I do beg to disagree, she said daintily, but let's us let Google have the final say, shall we? She produced an iPhone from within her petticoats.

Turns out they was both correct!

# OPEN FOR INSPECTION

**ME AND MAARTJE HAD SPENT** every Saturday for like six months looking at houses. The shittiest shitholes, mostly, or if they were good there'd be like a hundred people there, so many they had to send us through in groups, and you'd know you had no chance in hell of getting it. We bid at a couple of auctions where we thought we might just be able to afford one, but at the first auction the bidding flew right past our limit within two minutes and kept on flying, and at the second one the opening bid was exactly our limit. But we continued to spend every Saturday looking. Cause what else were we gonna do? And then we'd go home in the afternoon and Maartje would crawl into bed, put the blankets over her head and wail, 'We're never going to find our home!'

So this one Saturday, it was around two or something and we were in the middle of our list for the day, it was like the third or fourth house out of about seven. We got to the place and there was the usual crowd gathering out front. Not a huge crowd at that one, maybe only fifteen or twenty people, cause it was nothing out of the ordinary; you could tell without even going inside that it would just be another damp, pokey, rotting, peeling, crumbling terrace with a long hallway down one side, a couple of bedrooms, a small worn-out kitchen, a decrepit bathroom out back, and a weird smell. And everyone was doing the usual thing of ignoring each other but secretly sussing each other out, like who's got money, who looks seriously interested, who might be a builder, that type of thing. You start to see the same people all the time, cause you're all looking in the same area and price range. But you don't really get friendly with them or anything; they are, after all, your rivals.

The agent wasn't there yet, five minutes late and counting. There's always a tight window between houses on your list, so everyone's pretty antsy to get in and out quick. When the agent is late, you have to make the call of whether the house has enough potential to make it worth missing the next one. A bunch of people decided that this one didn't and left, leaving maybe ten of us.

Then the rain started. That awful gloomy winter rain. At first just a few cold, fat drops, and people muttered in anger at the agent for stranding us out there, but then suddenly it got hard and everyone panicked. No-one had an umbrella, we hadn't expected to stand outside, we hadn't expected rain, we hadn't known what to expect.

But this one hipster couple who we'd seen a dozen times at other houses, and I'd always found them irritating, particularly the guy's weird earrings and carefully messed-up hair and habit of talking loudly to his spouse about all the termite damage and dry rot – an old trick, nobody falls for it – and, well, I had to review my opinion of them, 'cause they had a big old van and they just threw open the back doors and called to us all to jump in.

So we went from like adversaries competing for the same houses to comrades-in-arms, united in our hatred of the common enemy, that being the real estate agent. We all huddled together in that old van while rain pounded on the roof, talking quietly about whether anyone had put in an offer on the Silver Street house, bemoaning the cost of houses generally, and inveighing against real estate agents, with particular emphasis on the current one who was late.

And then, through the dirty rain-streaked windows, we saw a small, brand-new sports car come screaming up the street and stop in front of the house. The vanity number plate said 'KASH'. The downpour was just petering out. A very young man climbed out of the car, opened the boot and pulled out an 'Open for Inspection' sign, which he deposited on the footpath outside the house. His hair was moussed up into a small faux-hawk and he bore an expression of long-suffering disdain. His suit was expensive but not classy, and his Rolex was chunky and highly conspicuous. He didn't seem surprised that nobody was waiting to see the house; in fact, he didn't seem like he cared about anything. As we all piled out of the van, he pulled out a large set of keys and climbed the steps towards the front door.

We filed through the gate and followed him up the steps. When he noticed us, he snapped, 'Wait on the footpath, please! I need to open up the house!'

We obediently backed down the steps and stood just outside the gate, peering through the open front door as he disappeared down the hallway. We heard him speaking to someone inside. His voice was raised, he sounded angry. After a minute, he returned, shaking his head in exasperation.

He gave us a curt nod to indicate that we were now permitted to enter and view the house. But as we climbed the steps he said, 'The tenants are home. They were supposed to be out for the inspection, but they're here.' This strange new piece of information slowed but did not stop our progress towards the door. It was no longer just an empty house we were entering, though; now we were intruding in someone's space, and none of us were quite sure how to feel about that.

The house smelled like eggs. One after another, we stuck our heads into the front bedroom and looked it up and down, noting peeling paint on the ceiling, damp patch on the wall, small size of the room. There was no need to even physically enter the room; all necessary information could be gathered from a simple glance in, up and down. We then processioned down the hallway to the second bedroom and gave it the same cursory looking-over. The sound of a television was audible from deeper within the house, along with some sort of air hose sound, and the egg smell increased in intensity.

As the hallway disgorged us into the large back room, which had been created by knocking out the wall between what had once been the lounge room and dining room, we beheld an old man sitting in a wheelchair, covered in blankets, with an oxygen tube connecting him to some sort of machine. Standing behind him with a hand on his shoulder was a grey-haired woman, her jowls and cheeks sagging under the weight of the world; the term 'care-worn' came to mind. They both observed our arrival with silent, baleful stares. We stopped, the ten of us banking up just inside the doorway, not game to intrude further on this sad tableau. We stared at the old couple, and they stared back.

The agent, from his position in the open front doorway at the other end of the hall, noticed the log jam-type situation and called to us angrily, 'Just ignore them! They weren't supposed to be here! Go ahead and look through the house!' The hipster couple were first to move. They sidled cautiously through the room, passing between the old couple and the television, murmuring a quiet apology as they tiptoed on into the kitchen. Maartje and I went next. I tried to regain my cynical, appraising eye, noting where the floor felt a bit bouncy, observing that the stove was electric, not gas, and that you had to go outside to get to the toilet. But my attention was continually drawn to the couple, and to their pitiful existence in this grubby, worn out house. Whoever bought the place would have to be the ones to evict them. That, really, was the unspoken message here. They knew it, and now we knew it too. It was no mistake that they were home during the inspection.

After a cursory walk around the small back garden, our group filed back through the house and out the front door. The agent didn't even bother taking down our names, and nobody asked for a copy of the contract. We all just said 'thanks' flatly as we exited, nodded to each other and went our separate ways.

'What did you think?' asked Maartje as I started the car.

'Pretty run down,' I said.

'Could be cosy though, with some fresh paint.'

'There was some rising damp in those front rooms.'

'Could get that fixed.'

I drove slowly down the street and turned the corner.

'Maybe we should have got a contract,' Maartje said.

'Do you reckon?' I asked. 'What about that old couple, though? Whoever buys that place will have to kick them out! How shitty would that be?'

'It would be very shitty,' she conceded. 'But just imagine finally having a house! Imagine having our Saturdays back! Imagine this fucking nightmare being over! We could spend our time picking out paint colours, and planting a garden, and oiling outdoor furniture, instead of this.' She leaned back in her seat, almost in tears.

I could see her point. To be done with house hunting, to settle down somewhere and be free to start our lives. Be grown-ups.

Have children, perhaps. Grow old. But then I thought of the couple. They had grown old, and now they would lose their home.

But the thing was, it was going to happen anyway. Somebody was going to buy that house and kick them out, and fucking hell it might as well be us. It would be seriously fucked, kicking them out, and we'd feel like horrible people. But we'd soon forget that bit. That was just the way the world worked. What can you do in this life but play the cards as they are dealt?

'You're right. Let's go back and get a contract,' I said. I circled around the block and came back up the street.

As I pulled up to the house, the hipster couple were just getting out of their van. And then I spotted another one of the couples climbing out of their Subaru across the street. I double-parked, put the blinkers on, and Maartje and I jumped out. We all converged at the gate. Nobody said anything. We avoided eye contact.

The real estate agent, that smug little fucker, was standing in the doorway, smirking, holding a stack of contracts, ready for us.

# HOW TO INSTALL

IT IS ONE OF THOSE CLASSIC Sydney winter days: deep blue sky, couple of clouds drifting softly along, sun gently warming the brick houses of a typical Inner West street, the kind with trees in the roadway (camphor laurels, in this instance), their middles pruned out to avoid power lines. Cars are parked between the trees: mostly Japanese imports, some Australians, a couple of Europeans. The verge's grass is radiant green thanks to the weeks of bountiful rain that always precede winter proper, and the gardens are dizzy with flowering shrubs. Except at one house, which features a wide, sparse, well-kept lawn populated only by a few rose bushes pruned back severely for winter. Along the edge of the verandah, a few garden gnomes chase each other in frozen motion. In front of this house, sitting on the kerb in a wide space between two parked cars, a bald man in his thirties, beard but no moustache, dark-blue shorts, light-blue work shirt, bare legs splayed out in front of him, peers intently down at a small white booklet on the ground between his legs. In his hands, held up and slightly off to one side so as not to obstruct his view of the booklet, is the cistern of a toilet, from which protrudes a small length of PVC pipe surmounted by a black O-ring. From the car to his left, a white

Holden wagon, comes the muffled sound of a radio sports report. Up at the side of the house, at the end of the driveway, behind a fence, a small chocolate Lab and a white Maltese Terrier lie in the sun, half dozing and half keeping an eye on things. A jet, just taken off from the airport, roars overhead, then fades to quiet as it lofts its way to somewhere in the distance. Somewhere far, no doubt.

# FLEAS

BABY GISELLE FELL ASLEEP two minutes before they pulled in to the Ikea car park. Wouldn't you know it? All afternoon they'd been trying to get her to go down for her nap, and of course now, when they'd given up and decided to go to Ikea, she was out. It was Lanie who craned her neck around and noticed. 'She's asleep,' she said to Josh.

'Oh, crap,' said Josh.

'I can stay in the car with her.'

'Nah, I'll stay with her. You go in. You've got a better idea of what we need.'

Josh found a shady spot at the far end of the car park and Lanie got out. 'If she wakes up, you guys come and find me. I'll keep my phone where I can hear it.'

Josh watched as Lanie made her way across the vast expanse of car park. Then he got out his phone and played Marble Mountain. At the end of each level, he glanced up to take in the goings-on in the car park — not that there was much going on, really — and checked to see if Giselle was still sleeping. Giselle was indeed still sleeping, her head lolling at an uncomfortable-looking angle, mouth open, long strand of drool slowly darkening her shirt.

On one glance up, Josh noticed a couple near the main entrance having what looked to be a rather heated discussion. The woman was heavily pregnant and resting her arms on a shopping trolley piled high with flat packs while the man gestured and shouted. Josh watched them with some amusement for half a minute, but was interrupted by a great big sigh from Giselle. He looked around but she was still asleep so he went back to Marble Mountain.

When he finished the next level and glanced up again, Josh observed something quite unusual. In fact, he wasn't quite sure what to make of what he was seeing. Several black-clad figures in masks were approaching Ikea from various points around the car park, all holding what appeared to be semi-automatic machine guns. Every now and then they signalled to each other with cryptic, precise, emphatic hand gestures. Was this some kind of marketing stunt? Or some sort of activist street art piece? Maybe a film shoot? Josh looked around to see if there was a camera crew on the periphery, or if, in fact, anyone else was even noticing this strange tableau. But the car park was empty of people at that moment, with the exception of the couple by the entrance, too engrossed in their argument to notice anything else. Josh seemed to be the only witness to this mysterious event.

It did not cross Josh's mind that the men in masks might actually be for real until one of them gunned down the arguing couple. The pregnant woman was thrown backwards, landing in a sad, motionless heap. The man sprawled forwards onto the trolley of flat packs, then slumped onto the ground and was still.

Josh's heart was pounding, though he still could not quite believe what he was seeing. The black-clad figures now moved rapidly into the store, and Josh could hear gunfire and screaming inside. For several seconds he remained completely frozen, then with trembling hands he rang Lanie. Maybe he could warn her, get her to find a way out the back. Her phone rang and rang. 'Fucking answer!' he shouted. It occurred to him that more gunmen might be roaming the car park, so he slid down in his seat and peered around cautiously.

*Hi this is Lanie, I'm not available to take your call at the moment—*

'Shit!' Josh ended the call and tried again. It rang and rang. 'Lanie! Fucking answer your phone!' he roared. Startled awake, Giselle spluttered and began to cry. Josh looked around at her. 'Shhh, baby,' he said distractedly.

*Hi this is Lanie—*

He hung up. He had no idea what to do. Run in and try to save his wife? He would certainly be shot. And he couldn't leave Giselle alone in the car. But could he just sit here and watch as his wife was killed? He considered starting the engine and flooring it across the car park, smashing through the front door of Ikea. But what would that accomplish, exactly, other than getting both him and his baby killed?

He checked the news on his phone to see if there was any information about what was going on, but there was no mention of it. Surely this would be breaking news, if this was real. He tried Lanie again but got her voice mail. A few minutes had passed with no further sign of activity at the door. Only the murdered couple's bodies lying on the footpath kept Josh from concluding he had imagined the whole thing.

Then he heard sirens in the distance and immediately felt a

tremendous sense of relief. The authorities were here! They would fix this. He and his wife and baby would all be home together for dinner, laughing and shaking their heads and saying, 'Well now wasn't *that* a crazy day!'

A police car came screaming into the car park, followed shortly by another. More sirens wailed in the distance. A helicopter appeared overhead and remained there, hovering. A police truck pulled in.

There was then an explosion from inside Ikea, shattering all the front windows and sending debris flying. The car rocked a bit on its springs from the pressure wave. The shock escalated Giselle's crying to shrieking. Smoke began pouring out of the building.

Josh tried to visualise the situation inside. It was certainly possible that plenty of people had survived that explosion. It was an enormous store, and there were lots of places to hide and take shelter. All those mock-ups of bedrooms and kitchens. Cabinets and wardrobes and modular sofas. Lanie would have found a safe place to hole up somewhere at the back. The Skågtorp, for instance, was quite sturdy, and could certainly have withstood the blast; she was probably waiting it out inside one of those. The cops would go in and kill all the gunmen, and then Lanie and everyone else would emerge from their hiding places and everything would be alright. They'd take Giselle to a playground and get ice-cream cones and laugh when Giselle got ice-cream all over herself, as she always did.

The cops didn't seem to know what to do, though. They had parked their cruisers in front of the store, but were huddled behind the cars, conferring frenetically. Many of them were wearing shorts, which struck Josh as odd. A few more cop cars pulled in, and then a couple of large four-wheel drives with flashing lights but no markings. A second helicopter joined the first one overhead.

There was a second explosion and a frenzy of gunfire from inside the store. Josh reloaded the news on his phone and there it was. Breaking news:

> ### TERROR AT IKEA.
> *Reports that a number of gunmen have stormed Ikea. Explosions have been heard. Confirmed fatalities. More to follow.*

He dropped the phone on the passenger seat and closed his eyes. Giselle was now hysterical, sobbing so hard she was almost choking. Although Josh was vaguely aware that he should be comforting her and calming her down, his body seemed to have forgotten how to move. But you know how they have all that stuff at the end, at Ikea, that whole giant section you have to walk through on your way to the checkouts, where they have all the frying pans and bathmats and picture frames and packs of thirty AAA batteries and closet organisers and cushions and melon ballers and those whimsical decorative metal animals on spikes that you can put in your garden and placemats and clocks and area rugs and storage solutions and curtain rods and mirrors and baskets and finger puppets and drinking glasses and packs of coat hangers and pitchers and printed fabric and cheese graters and wine glasses and scented candles and garden chairs and all that sort of stuff? Well, maybe Lanie just got caught up in looking at all the stuff in that section. That was why she was taking so long. Any minute he'd hear her footsteps approaching the car, he'd hear the boot open, the crinkling of bags as she loaded them in, the slam of the boot shutting. And then she'd get in, she'd calm Giselle down, and they'd drive home. On the way she would tell him all the things she bought and the plans she had for organising Giselle's toys so the house wouldn't be so cluttered, and when they got home they'd put away the laundry – always so much laundry – and start thinking about dinner. Oh, and give the cat his flea treatment. Those damn fleas are so hard to get rid of!

# RIGHTS OF MAN

I HAD BEEN PLAYING *Doctor Panda's Airport* on the iPad but then I needed to do a wee, so I told my dad. He said we'd put the iPad on the table and go and do a wee and when I came back I could play *Doctor Panda's Airport* some more. So we went to the toilet and I did a wee and then we came back but then my mum said dinner was ready and I had to sit on the chair and they said I couldn't play *Doctor Panda's Airport*. I got quite upset, not so much about playing *Doctor Panda's Airport* but because I had been told one thing and now was told another. I had expected to return from doing a wee to play *Doctor Panda's Airport* some more and instead had returned from doing a wee to be told I could not play *Doctor Panda's Airport* anymore but rather had now to sit on a chair and eat dinner. I don't even like sitting on a chair and eating dinner, especially when that dinner is peas.

So I cried. Because I cannot abide injustice. When it is wrought against me, I mean.

They tried to calm me down. They soothed, they coaxed, they comforted, they pleaded. But I kept on crying. So then they got annoyed. They got stern. They cajoled, they ordered, they commanded, they shouted. But obviously none of that was going to right the wrong that had been done to me. So I kept on crying.

Then my dad offered a deal. 'Okay, listen. How about this: you can play for a few more minutes, but after that we're putting away the iPad and you're going to sit on your chair and eat your dinner, okay? And I don't want to hear any more crying.' That seemed reasonable, inasmuch as it involved my getting to play *Doctor Panda's Airport* some more, so I nodded. He took out his telephone. 'How many minutes should we let you play?' he asked. I held up some fingers. I'm not sure how many, but I generally hold those fingers up in these sorts of situations and it usually seems to be a reasonable response. And in this case also, for my dad said, 'Three minutes? Okay, I'm setting my timer.' He did something on his telephone and then placed it on the table beside me. 'When the timer rings, the iPad goes away and you come and eat dinner and no more whinging or crying. Okay? Do we have a deal?' I nodded.

He handed me the iPad and helped me get back to *Doctor Panda's Airport*.

And so the grown-ups sat at the table eating and talking and I played *Doctor Panda's Airport* some more. Although actually, to tell you the truth, it was quite a generous allocation of time, and I was pretty sick of *Doctor Panda's Airport* by the time the telephone finally made noise. It had always been about the principle of the thing, not about playing *Doctor Panda's Airport* per se. So I was all too happy to put away the iPad and do something else. They have this round thing in that room with lots of marbles on it that is pretty interesting. I ate a couple of bites of dinner, just to placate them, and then went to play with that.

# POIOUMENON

**SO LIKE THIS GUY**, while waiting for the train and listening to a podcast about a guy whose appendix burst and while he was in hospital a trainee nurse pulled out his breathing tube unsupervised and destroyed his oesophagus and he was deprived of oxygen for ten minutes and suffered severe brain damage and his girlfriend who later married him takes care of him and after years of determination and hard work he can at least smile again sort of and make a bit of a noise and they got him this device he can use to indicate if he's hungry or thirsty or cold and they have a blog about their story and they got a special van to get his wheelchair around in and they want to inspire other people facing hardship to believe in themselves and know that if they work hard they can overcome anything, he, the guy listening to that story and waiting for the train on his way home from work, feels a pang of envy, of actual envy for either the brain-damaged guy or his girlfriend, not envy for having brain damage or having your partner incur brain damage but for the fact that they evidently don't have jobs, presumably some kind of litigious settlement or insurance payout from the hospital for the negligence resulting in serious harm would support them fairly well considering they can afford a special van and communication device and also their own apartment with special accoutrements and accommodations for his differently-abled state and condition, and not only they don't have jobs but they have a story, an uplifting story that they go around telling and it gets them on the radio and all kinds of people write to them to say thank you and God bless you and what an inspiration and their lives aren't just day after day of mundane meaningless labour and toil and drudgery and routine, and the oesophagus guy had been in Iraq, it was very dangerous and full of Improvised Explosive Devices, but he made it home in one piece and he had his whole life ahead of him but then the appendix thing happened and the oesophagus thing and the brain damage thing and even after that his father died in a car accident and his mother committed suicide and his brother went to prison for twenty years and seriously how much worse could things get for a person but nevertheless the guy waiting for the train has this fleeting thought that in some way maybe the oesophagus guy's life is somehow actually preferable to his own, but then he feels really guilty and like a total asshole for thinking that, like it's one of those sort of sick-guilty things that pass through your head sometimes and really you are just being a totally self-pitying fuckhead because you have a job and a house and a wife and a baby and a great life that 99 point 9 percent of the world wishes they had and yet you are envying someone who has had so many terrible things happen to him it's not even funny, just because you are tired and your job kind of sucks. It's a pretty fucked-up thing to think, and the guy knows it's fucked up, even as he thinks it. But it should also be mentioned here that the guy, the one waiting for the train and listening to the podcast, is also possessed of a proclivity to write, as in of a literary bent, I won't use the term 'aspiring writer' to spare you the cliché but also because he really has no aspirations; writing is just his wont, a thing he does, so at the same time as he's having this fucked-up feeling of envy for the oesophagus guy and subsequent guilt over having the fucked-up feeling of envy, he's also thinking about how maybe there could be a story in there somewhere, and trying to think how you could make that work. It couldn't just be a story about a guy waiting for the train, listening to a podcast and feeling envy and then guilt; that would just be prosaic and jejune. It would need something more; it would need to be repackaged and retooled in some way to give it more layers, more depth, to make it more literary, so to speak. It should be explained here, however, that a few years previously the guy (the one waiting for the train) had come to feel like everything w/r/t writing had been done before and anything he tried was just rehashing the same old shit and he got kind of bored with and sick of fiction, both writing and reading it, and as a result his inclination to write had ebbed in a big way. But then he'd discovered the writer David Foster Wallace and in a short space of time had read everything David Foster Wallace had written. Now, you may already know this, but although often referred to as a postmodern writer, and certainly descended from that literary lineage and heavily influenced by it, he, David Foster Wallace himself, was actually very much of the opinion that postmodernism, while groundbreaking and radical in its heyday, had, by the time he, David Foster Wallace, had come along, well and truly run its course; that the deployment of techniques such as deconstruction of traditional narrative structure and intertextuality and metafiction and irony, which techniques had made postmodernist literature so revolutionary in the sixties, had now become so commonplace that postmodernism had essentially become exactly the mainstream norm that it had initially sought to depose. In essence, David Foster Wallace was calling for a new literary movement, one that evolved beyond the cynicism and hipness and ennui of postmodernism, that was willing to take risks and be heartfelt and naïve and wide-eyed and sentimental. And yet he knew that the clock could not be turned back; postmodernism had left its mark on the cultural landscape and whatever new form literature took would have to concede that. And therein lay the crux of David Foster Wallace's conundrum: is it possible to be cynical and naïve at the same time? But then also David Foster Wallace has this distinctive voice in his writing, this kind of persona that draws you in, makes you feel like you really know him, like he is speaking intimately and familiarly directly to you, the reader, which actually was another big thing of his, that the voice in writing was very important because writing's main job was to make the reader feel, if only for a short time, a bit less alone in the world. Which says a lot about David Foster Wallace, maybe. But anyway, the point here is that his writing voice is really engaging and funny and witty and likable and, to an aspiring writer, really hard not to totally copy, no matter how hard he or she might try not to. It's like reading David Foster Wallace ruins you forever as a writer, because it becomes impossible to not always forever after sound like a person trying hard to write like David Foster Wallace, only not, obviously, anywhere near as well. I don't mean just in terms of the congenial voice, but also his stylistic quirks, for e.g. the deployment of long dense blocks of text without paragraph breaks, the explaterative run-on sentences, the pleroma of obscure vocabulary words, the use of abbreviations and acronyms, the *intus libri* inclusion of Latin phrases, the juxtaposition of colloquial idioms with Byzantine phraseology.[1] So in a way, and this is

---

1. And, of course, the extensive use of footnotes, sometimes rambling on for pages, even to the point of taking over from the main text for a while and becoming entirely separate stories, creating the sense of listening to one of those cool sorts of friends who always gets tangled up in their thoughts and sidetracked by tangents for a while before finally, eventually, coming back to their initial conversational thread.

sort of a twisted irony, David Foster Wallace, who wanted to help move fiction out of the quagmire of postmodern too-cleverness and set it free, kind of fucked fiction writing up forever because everything anybody writes now stands in the shadow of his work. Or maybe that's just for the one guy, the one waiting for the train and listening to the podcast about the oesophagus guy and then feeling envy, and then feeling guilt, and then thinking there could be a story in that and wondering how you'd make it work, and then thinking about how David Foster Wallace would have thought of a way because David Foster Wallace had a particular talent for exactly that, he has many stories in which we the reader are privy to the thoughts of a character that is somewhat repulsive and pondering some inner thought or desire that we can all relate to a bit, just a bit, though, and in his stories David Foster Wallace makes it kind of extreme, which is cool because you think, yeah I do know that thought or feeling but I'm nowhere near as fucked up as this guy, but anyway the point is that the man waiting for the train, as he's thinking how would David Foster Wallace use that scenario to make a good story (or whatever you want to call it, the word 'story' seems hardly apt since the stuff he does sort of breaks a lot of narrative conventions, but to call them 'pieces' sounds really pretentious), he realises that whatever he does is going to end up sounding just like some guy being a David Foster Wallace wannabe, ripping off David Foster Wallace's unique and distinctive style without the brilliance and cleverness and keen wit and loveable humour and staggering vocabulary, and then the man thought maybe the piece could work if he made it ragingly self-aware of its being a total rip-off/paean/homage to David Foster Wallace, like twisting the whole thing around and being like, 'yeah I know I am trying to be David Foster Wallace, ha *hah*, that's the whole point, look at me trying to ironically be just like David Foster Wallace', which he thought might be something David Foster Wallace might try, if he weren't famous and were in the position the man was currently in, which would mean David Foster Wallace wasn't famous but someone else was famous for the exact same thing David Foster Wallace is actually famous for in the real world. And he wasn't sure whether David Foster Wallace would approve of his efforts w/r/t trying to use irony and self-awareness doubling back on itself in this way to solve the conundrum or if David Foster Wallace would think it was a terrible idea and so unbelievably and preposterously postmodern and metafictiony and exactly the sort of thing he (David Foster Wallace) had been trying to get the hell away from, and would hate. But he (the man waiting for the train) thought it might be good to at least try it out anyway and maybe even send it to David Foster Wallace to see what he (David Foster Wallace) thought, except he couldn't, because David Foster Wallace was dead, and actually, really, that was the saddest part of the whole story.

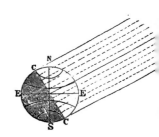

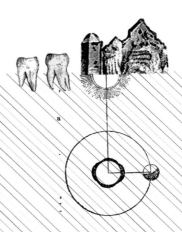

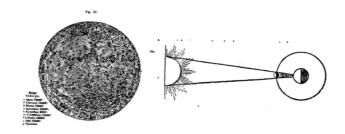

# TOOTH

**HE BRUSHED HIS TEETH** before going to bed. He brushed them good and hard. He brushed them so hard that one of them fell out. It fell into the sink. He sighed and leaned on the sink, looking down at it. The sink came loose from the wall and crashed to the floor, crushing both his feet and opening a large gash on his right ankle. He staggered out into the hall, where he stepped in a rusty bear trap, which snapped shut around his left shin, shattering the bone. After prising the bear trap open and extricating his leg, he hopped down the hall, his left leg dangling by a piece of sinew. He hopped through some broken bottles and tacks, causing him to fall sideways against the banister, which gave way and sent him tumbling down the staircase and onto the floor by the front door. As he lay there staring up at the hanging light fixture, it came loose from the ceiling and crashed down on his face, shattering into a million pieces and gouging out one of his eyes. He crawled out from under it and dragged himself back up the stairs, pushed open the bedroom door and crawled into bed next to the woman who hated him. She opened her eyes and looked at him for a moment, then mumbled something and rolled over back to sleep. He lay in the dark and with his tongue felt the space where his tooth used to be.

# CONTRACT

A CHANGE HAD ROLLED IN and by the time Bill got out of the cab at Canberra airport the wind was blowing pretty hard. He joined the other smokers for a last cigarette, all of them huddled together among swirling bits of rubbish, before going into the terminal. There was a long queue at the ticket counters. He found himself standing behind a large middle-aged man in a suit and stared with fascinated disgust at the deep crease in the back of the man's sunburned neck. It opened like a mouth whenever the man looked down at his watch and then closed back up again when he lifted his head. As the line moved, Bill kicked his carry-on bag along in front of him; it was stubborn and he really had to put his foot in to move it.

A not-very-friendly young woman with a blond ponytail and a lot of eye makeup handed him his boarding pass and directed him to Gate 14. On the way there he passed a men's room and thought it would be prudent to make use of it. It was crowded with businessmen. Bill pushed through them to get to the urinals, then hefted his carry-on bag over his shoulder and wedged himself between two of them. He stared straight ahead while he peed.

At the security checkpoint, Bill put his keys, cigarette lighter and coins in the plastic tub, which he placed on the conveyor belt along with his bags and then waited obediently at the metal detector. An imperious woman nodded curtly to him and he walked through it gently. It didn't go off. On the other side he picked up his bags and keys and was about to get on the escalator when a big uniformed Maori bloke motioned for him to come over. The bloke mechanically recited some spiel about testing for explosive residue that Bill didn't quite catch, but he understood what was expected of him so he nodded and put his bags on the table. The man rubbed a swab on the outside and then the inside of the bags and ran it through his machine. Then he did the same for Bill's clothes. Evidently the test came out negative. 'Awright, mate, John Howard can sleep soundly tonight,' quipped the bloke, probably for the fiftieth time that day. Bill snorted politely at his joke even though it wasn't funny.

At the top of the escalator was the departure lounge. Bill found a seat. He pulled a book out of his backpack and tried to read it, but found it difficult to concentrate. Instead, he watched the people around him and tried to listen to their conversations.

A group of people gathered next to him, some of them taking up the rest of the seats in his row and the rest of them standing. They were boisterous. He figured out that they were all travelling together for work, and had spent the afternoon having drinks. They were all a bit pissed, joking around with each other, wondering where missing members of their group were, showing each other photographs they'd taken during their adventures in Canberra and shrieking with laughter.

The ruddy man sitting across from Bill was talking on his mobile phone, speaking into a small piece of plastic affixed to a wire that dangled from his ear. He was enthusing about the contract for some analysis of research about an application under development to be discussed in the meeting the next day, and seemed to genuinely care about it judging by the way he punctuated his words with emphatic hand gestures that his interlocutor could not see. The man was reclined in his seat, legs splayed out in front of him, as comfortable as if he were lounging at home in his bathrobe on Christmas morning.

Bill looked around at all the people. So many beautiful women. What was it about women in airports? Bill watched one sad-looking woman for a long time, fascinated by the way her hair fell across her shoulders.

Men talking on mobile phones kept walking through his field of vision. They were all kind of scary. Bill felt self-conscious in his jeans and t-shirt. Nearly all the men were wearing suits and carrying briefcases and had expensive watches and an air of importance. He looked at the wedding rings on their hands and absentmindedly rubbed his finger where his used to be.

The women were all so nice and beautiful, but these were the men they loved. Men who knew who they were and what they wanted and didn't let anything get in their way to get it. Men who were self-assured, financially secure, driven, confident. Serious men. Pragmatists. Not men who still didn't know what they wanted to be when they grew up. Not men who got excited about stupid small things, or about anything at all, really. Not men who were full of impossible dreams of lives they could never have.

An announcement was made that Bill's plane would be delayed by twenty minutes.

Now Bill watched a fortyish woman in a soft cotton sundress over near the service desk. His heart ached with loneliness and longing, so he read some of his book to take his mind off things. It was a book of short stories and nearly every story involved a relationship breaking up, which made him feel both better and worse at the same time.

He checked his mobile phone again to see if he had any text messages. He'd had a fight over the phone with his girlfriend that morning, which had continued by text message throughout the day. Then she had stopped responding and there was still no message from her. He wasn't even sure anymore what the fight was about.

They announced that his flight was open so he switched off his phone and joined the throng of people heading through the gate, down the stairs and out onto the tarmac. It was raining and everyone got wet walking across to the stairs leading up to the plane. At the bottom of the stairs was a bin full of umbrellas, too late to be of use to anybody.

Bill got to his seat and discovered that he was in the middle of three. He shoved his carry-on bag into the overhead compartment and sat down, then immediately had to get up again to let the guy with the window seat get by. Bill sat back down and found himself sandwiched between two men in suits. In the three seats in front of him were three men in suits. He peered over the shoulder of the one in front of him to see what he was reading. It was a paper entitled, 'A Digital Awakening: Moving from the Help Desk Environment into the Total Workstation Solution System'.

Who the fuck were these people? They all had wedding rings, shiny ones, firmly wrapped around their fat fingers on their soft hairy hands. Wives to go home to, kids to tuck into bed, homes, family holidays to look forward to, mates to have round for a barbecue, careers. He would once have felt only contempt and pity, being younger and wiser and not part of their world. Now that he was closer to their age, he felt envy, and the fact that he envied these people made him sick.

He seemed to have missed something somewhere along the way. Was this how people were supposed to be? He'd always been determined to live an unconventional life and had assumed that somehow the Fates would guide him to a great destiny of fame and fortune. The exact nature of that destiny was always unclear, but it had seemed unquestionable that it would come about one way or another. The idea of a regular corporate job, a life in the suburbs, a mortgage and kids had horrified him.

Now that life was looking pretty good. He had wasted so many years getting drunk and playing in rock bands, working shitty jobs, living from payday to payday. His plan had been to write three books, make three films, record three albums, and then die by the age of thirty. He'd done none of those things, and that plan now seemed utterly ridiculous. What had he been thinking? He now found himself washed up on the shores of middle age with only a low-paying job and a broken marriage to show for it.

His plan – or lack thereof – seemed to have backfired rather spectacularly. Follow your dream, they said in all those books and movies. Be true to yourself. You can be anything you want to be. You're special.

Yeah. Right.

Bill picked up his book and tried to read some more. Anything to make his brain shut up.

The plane took off and there was a good ten minutes of shuddering and shimmying while it climbed up through the storm clouds. Bill thought about what if the plane crashed. That would show them, both of them. Then they'd feel sorry. His wife and girlfriend both.

He couldn't concentrate on the book, so he put it in the seat pocket in front of him and flipped through the in-flight magazine. It was full of ideas for great luxury holiday destinations, the best golf courses, gift ideas for the corporate executive who has everything, investment tips.

The flight crew had only served half the plane with snacks when the pilot instructed them to take their seats. They were beginning their descent into Sydney and it was going to be a bumpy ride. The plane came down out of the clouds and circled around the city once before coming in. The guy in the window seat was asleep, so Bill leaned across him to look out the window. He could see water but couldn't figure out where they were until he saw Leichhardt Market Town. Then they crossed Parramatta Road, then the train tracks, then Bill could see the water tower in Petersham. He could see the park where he and his wife used to walk their dogs. He could see his house.

It wouldn't be his house much longer. For three years he had worked tirelessly on that place. There wasn't a square centimetre he hadn't touched. He'd refinished floors, painted walls, repointed brickwork, knocked out a double-brick wall, put in a kitchen, cement-rendered a chimney, replaced window sashes, built a shed and planted a garden. He wondered how his trees were doing.

The plane came in low over Sydenham, crossed the container yards and touched down onto the wet runway. It did not skid, crash or burn. It just slowed down.

As the plane taxied to the gate, Bill turned on his mobile phone. There was a missed call from his wife. He was surprised and excited and wondered what it was about. Maybe she wanted to have dinner, finally talk about things. He'd moved out so they could work on the relationship, but as soon as he was gone she'd wanted nothing to do with him. He'd heard from some mutual friends that she was seeing someone else. But then again, so was he.

When he got off the plane he hurried to a pay phone and called her.

'I picked up the contract for the house from the real estate agent today,' she said. 'I need you to come over and sign it.'

That was it. Once that contract was signed, the house was sold and there would be no going back.

He needed to buy some time. Even if it was only a couple of hours. He said he'd just flown in from Canberra and needed to go to his apartment and have something to eat, that he'd call her after that.

He went outside and lit a cigarette. There was a very long queue for the taxis. Bill joined it and a man in a suit in front of him coughed in a not-very-subtle indication of his disapproval of the smoke. Twenty minutes later Bill was in a cab on the way to his shitty little apartment. He looked out the window and clutched his backpack to his chest. He wanted to go home, not just to his apartment, or even his house, but home. He just wasn't sure where the fuck that was, exactly.

# MORNING MEETING

'RIGHT, EVERYBODY, let's settle down please,' said Edgar. 'You've all had some time this morning to mingle and get to know each other a bit, and hopefully you've enjoyed some coffee or tea and delicious carrot cake at the refreshment table – big thanks to Martin for organising that – but it's time to get down to business.' Edgar looked over the rims of his glasses at Charlie and Dave, who were still talking. They stopped and Edgar continued. 'Okay. Now. The conventional way to carry out a kidnapping in Western countries has always been to kidnap someone quite prominent with a lot of money, and then demand a very high ransom. This invariably results in the kidnappers being caught. For one thing, kidnapping someone prominent attracts a lot of attention from both the media and the law. And demanding a high ransom is naturally going to make people balk at paying up and encourage them to seek alternate resolutions. Is everyone with me so far?'

There was a general murmur of assent around the room. So Edgar went on. 'In some countries – Haiti and the Philippines come to mind – kidnappings are carried out in a much more pragmatic fashion. They kidnap someone fairly average. Well-off enough to pay a decent amount in ransom, sure, but not anyone from a well-known family. Not anyone with power or connections. And they demand a reasonable amount as a ransom. Something people would be willing to just pay up rather than deal with the uncertainty and headache of the alternatives.' Edgar turned to the bespectacled man behind him. 'Ted, have you got those handouts?'

Ted nodded and went around the room handing a piece of paper to each person present.

'Ted is handing out a list of five hundred names. Each person on that list is just an average person from a middle-class background. They will never be expecting to be kidnapped, so they'll be easy to pick up. We're only going to demand a ransom of four thousand dollars from each of them, a very reasonable amount that will be pretty easy for their families to get together quickly and pay up. If each of those five hundred names yields four grand, we'll have two million dollars. Subtract from that about a hundred grand for operating costs and dividing what's left equally among fifteen of us, we will each walk away with over a hundred and twenty thousand dollars. Sure, it would be nice to make millions of dollars and retire to some tropical island, but does that ever really work out? In movies, maybe, but in real life? No. They always get caught one way or another. But we're aiming low, under the radar, setting achievable goals for ourselves. And a hundred and twenty grand isn't bad for four weeks' work. Now, are there any questions?'

Fiona raised her hand and Edgar nodded to her. 'Edgar, could you describe the logistical aspects of the operation for us? For example, where will these people be held? And how will the ransom money be collected?'

'Yes, thank you, Fiona, those are very good questions. First of all, the holding area. In the guise of a film production company, we will rent out a large warehouse down near the airport. I believe Ted is already working on that. It will provide us with the industrial kitchen and the toilet facilities that we will need. We are sourcing army surplus cots and bedrolls. We'll also need to set up some televisions and board games to keep people occupied. We will want to be able to accommodate about a hundred people at a time, rotating them through in about three or four days. As for collecting the money, we will have a number of collection spots in the form of locked boxes concealed in various spots along Foreshore Drive, each with a number allocated to it. When a ransom note is sent out, that number should be entered in the database against that person so it can be held until the money is collected. At that time the number will be released and can be used again. We don't want anyone going to put their four thousand dollars in the collection box and finding a wad of cash already there, now do we?'

Fiona raised her hand again. 'What's to stop our ... uh ... victims—'

'Let's call them clients,' said Edgar.

'Right, what's to stop our clients from going to the police once they've been freed? Or their families from going to the police while we're holding them, for that matter?'

'Very good question,' said Edgar. 'It is critical to this operation that we maintain a consistent image of menace. This is where our Marketing team comes in. The demeanour of all our communications – ransom notes, phone calls, and so forth – needs to elicit a genuine fear that harm will come to the clients if our instructions are not followed to the letter, which of course includes no police. This mainly applies to the families, and to the clients afterwards – we are expecting that while in our custody, our clients will experience a certain degree of Stockholm Syndrome, and we've hired a psychologist as a consultant to help our guards develop techniques to enhance that aspect. That will minimise escape attempts.'

There was a pause. Edgar cleared his throat. 'Are there any more questions?' People looked around the room but no-one had any questions. 'Alright, then, we'll divide into groups. I believe Ted has already assigned each of you to one. Can the kidnappers come over here with me? The guards will convene at that end of the room with Michael, and if the administration team could follow Ted, he'll take you to the computer in the office and show you the database. Thanks for your time, everyone, and I'm looking forward to working with all of you. Please feel free to email me if you have any questions or concerns along the way.'

# SYMPTOMS

'WALTER, IS IT?'

He nodded sombrely as he entered her office. They shook hands. 'I'm Megan Ngesi,' she said. She gestured towards the chair by her desk. 'Please, sit down.'

They both took a seat. 'So,' she said. 'What can I do for you today?'

'Doctor,' said Walter, 'there is something really wrong with me.' He began wringing his hands and jiggling his leg anxiously. 'I've got some terrible disease. I just know it.'

She gave him a reassuring smile. 'Alright. Take it easy now, Walter. Tell me what makes you think there's something wrong with you.'

'Well ... I'm not quite sure how to put this.' He leaned forward and lowered his voice. 'I have to ... you know. Um. Go to the bathroom a lot.'

'Right, okay, so you're having a bit of diarrhoea, then? Is that it?'

'No, no, it's not diarrhoea. It's just regular ... you-know-what, but ... often.'

'Okay, I see. And how often is often?'

'Pretty much every day! And I have to, you know, um, urinate several times a day.'

'How many times are we talking about?'

'I'd say ... three or four? Maybe even five sometimes.'

'Right, okay. Well, that's not really all that out of the ordinary.'

He shook his head. 'It's not just that, though. I'm also hungry all the time. And thirsty.'

'Can you be a bit more specific?'

'Well, when I wake up in the morning, I'm hungry, so I have something to eat. Then I go to work and within a few hours I'm hungry *again*! So I eat some more. And then a few hours after that, usually around the time I get home from work, bang! I'm hungry again! Seems like I spend a great deal of my time thinking about what to eat, making food, eating, cleaning up after eating, shopping for groceries ... it's like my life revolves around eating. Totally crazy. *And* I have to drink water all the time or I get incredibly thirsty. I'm talking several glasses a day!'

'Well, again, that's really not terribly– '

'Hang on, there's more! Another thing is, I'm tired a lot of the time. In the course of a twenty-four-hour day, I spend several hours in bed asleep. Usually about seven or eight. And even when I'm not sleeping, I sometimes still feel tired! *Surely* that's an indication that there is something very wrong with me?'

'Well, okay, tell me something: is this how you have always been, or have any of these things changed recently?'

'I don't know, really. I guess I never paid attention before, so it's hard to say.'

'Well, you do realise, don't you, that everyone is like this? All these things you have described are completely normal?'

'No, you don't *understand*, Doctor. There's more. Like, also: I breathe *constantly*.'

'You breathe.'

'Yes. I have tried to stop and I can't. Not even for a couple of minutes. It's like I'm addicted to air or something. Seriously. I think if I had no air, I would die. I've never actually admitted that to anyone before.' He clutched his head in his hands.

She glanced at the clock. 'Okay. And was there anything else?'

'Well, I'm pretty sure I have obsessive-compulsive disorder.'

She leaned back in her chair and tapped her pen on her knee. 'Mm-hmm. And what makes you think that?'

'I wash my hands several times a day. And I bathe and change my clothes often.'

'I'm going to take a guess here and say every day?'

'Yes! Just about every day! If I don't, I feel dirty!'

'Right. And? Is there more?'

'Well, my memory is pretty much shot.'

'Is it.' She rubbed at a scuff mark on her shoe.

'Oh, yes. For example, when I go grocery shopping, I always forget things. Coffee, laundry soap, there's always something. I have to write everything down. Make lists. But it doesn't stop there: people's birthdays, social events, meetings, appointments – I had to write down this appointment, otherwise there's no way I would have remembered it. That's how bad my memory is.'

'Well, my receptionist had to write down that you had this appointment this morning, otherwise we wouldn't have remembered it. That's just normal!'

He sighed heavily. 'You just aren't getting it, Doctor! Something is really wrong with me! I am scared a lot of the time.'

'Scared? How do you mean? Scared of what?'

'I don't know! Lots of things. The future, death, the meaninglessness of life, the vastness of the universe, the emptiness of being.'

'So just, like, existential angst?'

'Yeah, I suppose. Is that the medical term? Also, I get lonely if I spend too much time by myself. But at the same time I don't always feel like I am connecting with my friends and family. Sometimes I feel alone even when I am around other people. And I worry about whether I will have enough money to live on when I retire. I worry about whether my loved ones are safe. I worry about whether I left the oven on, whether I left the cat in or out, whether the weird noise my car is making is something I need to get checked out. All this worrying.'

'Everybody worries.'

'Do they?'

'Yes, absolutely. Listen. All these things you've described, they're all perfectly normal. Just part of being human.'

'Well, I've been human all my life, but I never really noticed them before.'

'Sometimes when you start noticing things, they appear to be more significant than they actually are. But I can assure you that you are completely normal.'

'I am?'

'Yes.'

He smiled through tears of relief. 'Well, that's great to hear. I can't even begin to tell you. Thank you so much!'

'That's alright,' she said, standing up and moving to the door. 'Just relax and try not to think so much, Walter. You'll be fine.' She opened the door.

'Goodbye, Doctor. Thanks again.' He rose and made for the door, then stopped. 'Actually, there's one other thing.'

'Trust me, Walter! You're fine!'

'Well, it's probably nothing, but I may as well ask you about it while I'm here. I've got a mole on my leg that's gone a bit funny.'

'Oh. Alright, let me take a look.'

He put his foot on the chair and rolled up his pant leg. 'Just here,' he said, pointing to a mole on his calf.

She bent down and examined it. 'Hmm,' she said.

'What do you think?'

She straightened up and closed the door. 'Why don't you sit back down, Walter?' she said.

# NORTHWEST PASSAGE

LATE THAT MORNING, when the peak hour traffic had thinned out, Maureen decided to make another attempt at finding a northwest passage to Stonefields Mall. She had been studying the most current maps and felt certain that a way through the Westhills district must lie somewhere between Baylors Road and the golf course. To find the passage would mean establishing a direct route from the eastern side of town to the mall without having to go through the city centre, cutting twenty minutes off travel time and securing Maureen's place in the history books.

The trip was a disaster from the start. As soon as they were on the Northern Expressway, Henry vomited all over Fiona, and Maureen nearly drove off the overpass as she twisted around trying to minimise the mess in the back seat. As they came off the motorway onto Elizabeth Drive, Fiona's bottle of apple juice fell onto the floor and spilled all over the CDs that were scattered down there. And Baylors Road, which by that time of day should normally have been fairly clear, was bumper to bumper traffic because of a charity cricket match at the showground, so that Maureen wasted fifteen minutes just getting from Queen Street to Tunhall Drive, where she intended to begin looking for the passage.

When she discovered a long straight road leading almost due west, she thought she'd found it – it was certainly wide enough to be a main thoroughfare cutting across town. But as she drove along it, it quickly dwindled down to a single lane and turned out to merely be an access road along the edge of a small nature reserve. It ended in a cul-de-sac surrounded by a copse of trees. Maureen had no choice but to turn around and make her way back to Tunhall Drive to continue the search further north.

By that point the children were getting cranky and saying they wanted to go home. Fearing a mutiny, Maureen tightened discipline, threatening to revoke television privileges for a week if order was not maintained. Food supplies were running low, and the children were sick of eating the stale biscuits from the glove box. Maureen reduced their apple juice rations to one sippy cup each, further fuelling the seditious talk in the back seat of the car.

She stopped by the roadside to speak to some locals, who spoke abstractly of a legendary great road that headed westward to a 'place of enormous car parks' but could offer no concrete information or directions. Maureen was sure that they were referring to the passage, and was convinced that she was very close.

But the afternoon wore on with no sign of it, and she knew she had to get home to start dinner, so she reluctantly abandoned the search and turned back. She vowed to try again as soon as she could organise another expedition. She just hoped she could convince her backers at home to support one more attempt, for she was certain that the next time around she would find the passage and at last take her place on history's stage.

# BUILDING

**WHO OWNS THE DESERT?** Ralph asked around but nobody seemed to know. Maybe he asked the wrong people. He had this funny idea: he wanted to see a super modern skyscraper all by itself out there in the middle of nowhere. Also, he had sixteen billion dollars in his bank account.

He talked to some construction companies about his idea. They thought he was completely nuts, but when you have sixteen billion dollars you can get people to listen to you anyway. He hired a construction company to build his building, and Ralph and the head of the company flew around the desert in a helicopter to pick out a spot. But one spot was as good as any other, really; it was all flat, hot, sandy and empty.

So construction got under way. It was actually surprisingly easy, since there were no other buildings to worry about, no underground cables or sewers to work around, no environmental impact study needed, no archaeological review, no city traffic to tangle with, no development applications to file. Getting the materials and workers out there was a bit expensive, but Ralph could afford it. He mostly used Hercules cargo planes and a couple of Chinook helicopters, with the really heavy stuff coming in on trucks. He had to have a ninety-kilometre road built to connect to the nearest paved highway so that the trucks could reach the construction site, as well a landing strip for the cargo planes.

He built a little caravan village for the workers, which everyone came to call Ralphtown. He hired caterers and built a dining centre where they served breakfast, lunch and dinner but there were snacks available if you got hungry at some other time. He had a pool put in so they could cool off after a long hot day. Some of the guys put together a band and played a gig in the dining centre every few nights. They called themselves Shazbot. Jojo the crane operator played the drums. They just played classic rock covers, but everyone seemed to enjoy it.

Meanwhile, the building progressed. Once the foundation was finished, the structure went up pretty quick. Ralph had opted for a fairly standard steel girder construction with glass cladding, which he thought would look cool as the desert sun moved across the sky. 'How tall you want this thing?' the structural engineer had asked him. Ralph just made up a number right then and there, seventy-two storeys. Why not?

His skyscraper would need power, so he had a big field of solar collectors put in several kilometres away and ran the cables underground to his building. It wouldn't really need all that much power, anyway; just enough for lights and air conditioning.

Plumbing was a bit more of a challenge. The building wasn't going to be occupied, but Ralph still wanted the bathrooms to work. He had a large underground septic system installed for waste, and put in an enormous water tank that took up the top four floors, which he had filled by truckloads of water.

'What do you want in the rooms?' the construction foreman asked him. 'Desks or something?'

Ralph was damned if he knew. 'Nothing, I guess,' he said, 'but we may as well lay some carpet.'

Finally the building was completed. The crane was taken down and whisked away on a big flatbed truck. Ralphtown was dismantled and all the workers went back home to wherever they'd come from. The construction company boss asked Ralph if he was satisfied. Ralph said he was, and the construction company boss shook his hand and flew off in his helicopter, leaving Ralph alone with his skyscraper.

He grasped the big chrome handle on the tall, stately glass front door, heaved it open, and was enveloped by a blast of air conditioning. The foyer had high ceilings, a marble floor and dark wooden walls with a few large abstract impressionist paintings hanging on them. Very classy. There was a guard's desk, unmanned of course. Ralph tried out the chair. It squeaked a bit but it was pretty comfortable.

He took the elevator to the fifty-eighth floor and walked up and down the hallway, sticking his head into some of the empty rooms. He was glad he'd opted for the carpeting. The view out the windows was pretty amazing, you could see really far. He took the fire stairs up to the sixty-first floor and walked around some more, but it was pretty much exactly like the fifty-eighth floor so he took the elevator down to the underground car park. It was kind of spooky down there without any cars so he didn't stick around. He went back up to the lobby and looked at the artwork for a while. Then he went out and got in his helicopter and flew about a kilometre away so he could look at his building from afar. It sure looked funny, this big modern skyscraper all by itself, out there in the desert. He sat in the helicopter looking at the building for a few minutes, then turned and headed for home. He still had fourteen billion dollars in his bank account. On the way, he had a funny idea for a skyscraper in the middle of the ocean.

# BOWLING

**WELL, A WHOLE BUNCH** of us went ten-pin bowling one evening. There was myself and Andy and Edis and Lacey and Donald and Helen. We bowled and bowled, and after a while we noticed that the balls we were bowling were failing to reappear via the ball-return chute. At the same time, we registered the fact that the ball rack a couple of lanes over from us was quite full. We somehow became convinced that our dearth of balls could be ascribed to a mischannelling of the ball-return mechanism. A few of us approached the neighbouring lane and vociferously laid claim to some of their balls, much to the consternation and bafflement of said lane's occupants. Having bowled those new balls, however, and them also not returning, we found ourselves once again faced with the ball-shortage dilemma. We resolved it by going around the bowling alley and collecting more balls from the racks along the walls, which we then proceeded to bowl. They, too, did not return. Finally, Edis approached the manager and informed him of the strange phenomenon of our disappearing bowling balls. The manager enjoined us to bowl no further, rushed off, and promptly the lights in our lane went out. However, Helen, whose turn it was, unaware that we had been ordered to cease all bowling until further notice and not noticing that our lane had gone dark, bowled a ball, which prompted the manager to reappear and verbally assault Edis, for it seems there lay grave danger to the mechanic behind the scenes, who was vulnerable to serious injury or even death from a waywardly-thrown bowling ball whilst repairing the ball-return mechanism. So we were already in rather poor standing with the management of the bowling alley when suddenly the lights in our lane came back on and bowling ball after bowling ball began pouring out of the ball-return chute. There seemed to be no end to the deluge of bowling balls. They rapidly filled up the ball-return rack and then began to overflow onto the floor, each newly arriving ball displacing an older one as it was disgorged from the ball-return chute. Soon bowling balls were bouncing and rolling all over the place, much like a comical out-of-control popcorn machine. Edis and Donald and I began grabbing bowling balls as fast as we could and ferrying them to the racks along the walls, but the balls were coming faster than we could clear them away. An announcement came over the loudspeaker calling for urgent assistance to lane twenty-three, that being our lane. Two employees of the bowling alley promptly came running with tall bowling-ball trolleys to assist with the rescue effort. 'What happened?' one asked incredulously as he stacked bowling balls onto his trolley. 'The balls weren't coming back so y'all just went and got more balls?' He shook his head in disbelief at our foolishness. The rest of the evening proceeded without further incident, although, I must admit, I bowled quite atrociously.

# SUMMIT

**HE TOOK HIS NEW GIRLFRIEND** down the south coast of New South Wales for a week. They stayed in a little holiday unit at Tuross Head. They were old friends from high school, who'd liked each other at the time but nothing had ever happened. They'd lost touch, a couple of decades had passed, they'd reconnected, they were both single, and so they started seeing each other. It made for a nice, romantic, better-late-than-never type story.

And now the world seemed bright and full of marvels, like the baby chickens in the back garden of the house next door, and a bakery down at the shops that made the best scones ever, and thus they were able to believe what they fervently wanted to believe: that their story was a good story.

They spent the days driving up and down the coast, exploring towns, beaches and national parks. They pored over the road atlas together, taking great delight in the names of places. Bingie Bingie Beach. Potato Point. Mystery Bay. Wagonga Inlet. Often a place would merit a visit from them based solely on its name.

Late one morning while they were having coffee and scones and examining the map, he pointed at a little triangle in the middle of Gulaga National Park. Mount Dromedary, it said next to it.

Leading up to it were a broken grey line and a letter P: an unsealed road and a parking area. From there, a dotted line with a little walking man icon indicated that there was a hiking trail. It looked like about a two-kilometre walk from the car park to the summit.

'How about it?' he said.

'Sounds good,' she said.

He drove as she held the map and navigated them through the convoluted network of dirt roads. It turned out to be more difficult than it looked on paper. They kept passing turn-offs, going in circles, finding confusing forks in the road and ending up in strange places, or else back in a place they'd just been. At last they spotted a small hand-painted sign pointing the way to Mount Dromedary, down a small road they'd previously missed. They followed it. The road was soft earth, not much wider than the car, with high embankments on either side. It wended its way up and down steep hills through a dense, magical forest. They had to ford a couple of creeks, slowing down to a crawl and carefully nudging the car over big rocks and through six-inch-deep water. He was getting a bit nervous about skidding off the road, or crashing into an oncoming car if one came, or breaking his axle on a rock. He'd never driven on such rough terrain and it was starting to seem like a bit more than he'd bargained for.

They drove on that road for quite some distance, getting further and further from civilisation. They didn't see any signs of other humans at all. Finally, they came to a great big dip in the road, beyond which it was so riddled with ruts and jagged rocks that there was clearly no way they could drive any further. There was a small grassy area by the side of the road. They parked there and looked at the map. Was this the parking area represented on the map by the letter P? They weren't sure, but probably. It certainly seemed like the end of the unsealed road, so it must be. And so from here on must be the start of the walking track. Two kilometres to the summit. They left the car and started walking.

At first, it was easy going. Flat, open country, bathed in dappled sunlight. They spotted a wallaby. The trees rang with the tinkling of a thousand bellbirds. It was beautiful, and their spirits were high. Far off up above them, the summit of the mountain loomed, shrouded in mist. It looked rather a long way off, but they'd measured it on the map and it was clearly only two kilometres from the car park. If that grassy area had indeed been the car park. They still weren't really sure.

After twenty minutes or so, they came to a gate, beyond which the trees closed in and the trail turned sharply uphill.

'You want to keep going?' he said.

She turned to him in surprise. 'Well, yeah. I mean, don't you?'

'Yes, of course,' he said.

It was a relentless uphill climb. There would be a straight steep run for fifty metres or so, then a switchback turn and another fifty-metre straight run. Switchback, straight run, switchback, straight run. Over and over, ever upward. He very quickly became exhausted and his lower back ached. At every bend he hoped desperately to round the corner and find that they had reached the summit, but it was always just another stretch of trail that lay ahead. She was much fitter than he was. She had no trouble at all, but he had to stop and rest every few minutes.

All around them, the bellbirds continued their racket. 'Plink! Plink! Plink!' Somewhere far away, higher up, a strange bird called over and over in a crescendo ending in near-hysteria: 'Woodoo-woodoo-woodoo-woodoo-WOODOO!' They walked on, up into the mist; their skin glistened with it. Every so often, they came across a marker that told them the name of a tree or a type of rock. The markers looked very old, text etched in brass. It didn't seem like any other humans had been along this way in quite some time.

He was sure they were almost at the top of the mountain. Two kilometres wasn't all that far, really. So he struggled on. She asked several times if he was alright, whether he wanted to turn back. He hardly felt able to continue, but he was embarrassed and didn't want to disappoint her.

'We've come this far!' he said, panting. 'We can't turn back now!' He just continued to hope at each switchback that they would have arrived.

A metal plate mounted on a large boulder explained that it was made of monzonite, and that outcroppings of it could be found in concentric rings extending from the summit at sixty-metre intervals. They passed a tree with a lichen-covered sign identifying it as a ghost gum. They'd left the bellbirds far behind now; their clamouring was still audible from lower down the mountain.

And then they rounded a bend and the ground levelled off. There was a large placard with a map. Information! That's what they needed! He was very relieved until he consulted the map and discovered that, as far as he could work out, they had only gone two of the *seven* kilometres to the top. 'Summit: four hours return,' it said. Four hours!

Then they noticed another sign that said, 'Mount Dromedary parking area. No four-wheel-drive access beyond this point.' *THIS?* This was the *car park*? They couldn't imagine how any motorised vehicle could possibly make it this far up such a steep and narrow track.

'I don't know if we should keep going,' he said. 'It's two o'clock now. It'll be dark before we get back.'

'I don't think it's as far as all that. It won't take four hours.'

'But look at the map! It's five more kilometres to the top!'

'I don't think that's what it says.'

'Of course it is! Right there: four hours return.'

'I think that means from the bottom.'

'No, it means from here!' It came out louder and angrier than he'd intended.

She spoke quietly. 'It's a seven-kilometre round trip, starting from the bottom. That is what the sign says.'

He stabbed a finger at the map. 'No, look right here. Seven kilometres is the distance one-way.'

'That isn't what it says.'

He spoke slowly, as if to a deaf person. 'There is another five kilometres to go.'

She opened her mouth to say something, but didn't.

Having not anticipated such a major trek, they had no food or water with them. He was already very thirsty. It would be dark in a few hours and they couldn't agree on what the map said about how much further it was. Would it really take four hours to get to the top and back? Should they keep going? He had never been this far from civilisation before. He looked at his phone: no reception. What if he fell down or got bitten by a snake? Was his car going to be okay parked down there at the bottom of the mountain?

His fretting must have been evident on his face because she sighed and said, 'Alright, look. We can go back if you want.'

He pondered it. 'Well,' he said reluctantly, 'let's just keep going and see how we go.' Of course, he knew that the further they went and the closer they got to the top, the harder it would be to make the decision to turn back.

And so it was back to the same arduous walking, a steep straight run followed by a switchback turn and then another steep straight run. He was really struggling now and had to stop every few metres. He was drenched in sweat, soaked from the mist, his heart was pounding, his back and legs were aching, and he was utterly exhausted. He could see her esteem for him lowering by the minute, and it made him sad.

And then he reached a point where he simply could not go on. He found a flat rock to sit on.

'Do you want to turn back?' she asked.

'Maybe,' he mumbled.

'Alright, well, look. I'm just going to walk up and look around the next bend. Be a shame if we turned back just before the top.'

She marched off up the hill and he sat there watching her go. What a pathetic slob he was. Wasn't it just a matter of having the will to do something in order to do it? Some kind of inner strength thing? Never say die? He jumped up and ran off after her. Fuck it. They were going up this goddamn mountain.

It was now two hours into their climb. Two hours of ceaseless uphill struggle. Finally they arrived at another placard, and learned from it that they were nearly there. According to its map, they only had to go a bit further along the path they were on and then take a right turn onto another path to make the final ascent to the summit.

A sign pointed the way. It said, 'Rainforest Walk'. It was no longer just misting, they were now walking through a light drizzle. Their clothes stuck to them and their stringy wet hair hung over their foreheads. The path was nearly level now, only a gentle uphill grade. Enormous tree ferns loomed everywhere. They were inside a cloud. They were very far from home.

Then they came upon a confusing sign. It indicated straight

ahead along the main path for the Rainforest Walk, but the word 'summit' was written on the back in faded letters. Behind the sign, the ground rose nearly vertically into a dense tangle of plants.

'That must be the path that leads up to the summit,' he said. 'It goes off to the right, like on that last map.'

She pushed her way through the undergrowth and climbed up a ways, then came back down. 'I don't think that's a path. It might well lead up to the summit, but we really don't want to get ourselves lost up here. We'd better just stick to the track we're on.'

So they continued along the Rainforest Walk, admiring the ferns and vines and remarking on how eerily quiet it was. There didn't seem to be any wildlife up there, not even bugs. They couldn't hear the bellbirds down below anymore either.

Then something strange. The path levelled off and began to go downhill. They stopped. Was this the summit? Surely there would be a sign if it was. No, this couldn't be the summit; there was still a whole lot of mountain to their right, towering over them. Maybe this was only a brief downhill bit and the path would turn uphill again around a bend. They continued on but the path began sloping even more downhill. They were definitely heading back down the mountain. They stopped again. Well, maybe that had been the summit back there. Perhaps what was considered to be the summit wasn't the literal summit of the mountain, but just the highest point on the path?

They went back to where the trail levelled off and stood there for a while.

'This can't be it,' he said.

'But there's nowhere else to go,' she said.

They decided to just call this the summit. They'd gotten very close, at least. They could say that they'd been up the mountain. So they started back. After a few minutes, they came to the confusing sign again. That word 'summit' written on the back.

'Maybe it *is* pointing up this way,' he said. He pushed through the vegetation and scrambled up the hill a ways, and then he found a few steps made of rocks slotted into the earth. 'Steps!' he called down to her. 'I think this is the way!'

Invigorated by this discovery, he started climbing as fast as he could. She followed behind. There were no more steps, but there was a vaguely discernible path to follow. It was almost a vertical climb; they had to grab hold of trees and pull themselves up, going from rock to rock. A couple of times they couldn't see the path anymore and had to guess which way to go. Finally, they came to a point where they could see no more path. They stood on a rock, surrounded by a wall of bush.

'So is this the top?' he asked.

'I don't know,' she said. 'There's no sign, that's the weird thing. There ought to be a sign at the top. I just don't want to stray off the path and get lost up here, we'd be seriously screwed. You stay here and I'll check around.'

She ploughed off through the bush and disappeared. A minute later she called out, 'I found the sign! It's the summit!'

He hurried after her, and stepped into a clearing. It was the summit of a mountain, just like he'd seen in movies.

It was misty, but also bright. There was a big sign that said, 'Welcome to Summit'. There was a tall post with a metal seal on top of it, placed there by the Department of Geographical Surveying. All around the post was a large pile of rocks, added to by each climber who'd reached this spot over the years.

They took photos of each other and used the timer to take one of them together. They laughed at how bedraggled they looked in the pictures. Drenched and exhausted.

Then, aware that darkness would be arriving soon, they headed back down. Back on the Rainforest Walk, they caught a glimpse of a large dark-coloured bird hurrying through the bush. It looked like a large brown chicken. They hadn't seen any birds up there at all, and now here was this one.

It had taken them two and a half hours to reach the summit. It took less than one hour to get back down. It was so steep that they had little choice but to run, stumbling and nearly out of control, from switchback to switchback, until they reached the bottom. Back among the bellbirds.

He was really glad to see the car.

Back at the holiday unit, he found a book about Australian birds on the bookshelf. They flipped through it and decided that they'd seen a lyrebird – a rare sight, apparently, as they are very shy.

After that, things went sour. Maybe it was the argument at the map. Or maybe they had been kidding themselves all along. In any case, a couple of weeks after they got home, they called it quits.

# 4 goths at the late nite petrol station window

the bangladeshi comes to the window with the wrong chips again
so the girl leans forward, her mouth to the speak hole:
   *SEA* SALT FLAVOUR
   IT'S A *BLUE* BAG
he shuffles back to the shelves
   THIS GUY IS A FUCKING *RETARD*
the others laugh and nod
the artificial lights shine down upon them
they are right at home

now he returns with the right chips
so she leans in again:

    *AND* I WANT AN ESPRESSO DARE

he stares at her

    AN ESPRESSO *DARE*? IT'S A *MILK*?

off he goes again, shaking his head

    CAN YOU *BELIEVE* THIS GUY?

the boy at the rear pipes up:

    JUST WAIT TILL HE FUCKS UP MY FREEZIE
    I'LL MAKE HIM GO BACK AND FIX IT

the man behind the glass has returned
he is holding a carton of regular whole milk
the girl splutters in exasperation

    OH JUST FUCKING *FORGET* IT

# EXPOSURE

'SERIOUSLY,' HE SAID. 'I THINK I'M BLIND!'

'You're not blind,' she told him. 'It's just really dark.'

'I can't see anything. Nothing at all. I'm moving my hand around and I can't make anything out. Can you see my hand moving?'

'No,' she said.

'Well, maybe you're blind too!'

'That would be quite a coincidence, if that were so.'

They were quiet for a while, listening to the rapid ticking of the engine as it cooled.

'Are we upside down?' he asked. 'I can't even tell.'

'I don't know,' she said. 'On an angle, I think.'

'I guess when you can't see, it's hard to tell which way is up.'

'Yeah. That is true on so many levels,' she said quietly.

'What do you mean?' he asked.

'Nothing,' she said.

'I just felt something drip on me,' he said, alarmed.

She didn't answer.

'Something is dripping on my neck! It might be petrol or something!'

There was a frantic shuffling sound.

'What's that noise?' she asked. 'What are you doing?'

'Trying to see if I can free my legs,' he said. 'Or open the door. It's stuck.'

'Yeah. You said that before.'

From somewhere far above them, there came the sound of a truck barrelling past. It dwindled into the distance.

'It's getting really cold,' he said.

'Yeah.'

'How long do you think it will take for someone to come?'

'Could be quite a while,' she said. 'Unless you can find your phone.'

'I don't know where it ended up. It was in my pocket but I think it's down on the floor somewhere. Or up on the floor somewhere. Or wherever the floor is now. How long's quite a while?'

'Nobody knows where we are. Nobody knows we're together. Nobody knows we're down here. So, at least until the sun comes up. Maybe longer. I don't know how visible we are from the road. If at all.'

'But we might freeze to death!'

'It's not that cold.'

'Can you reach the horn? Does the horn work if the car's not running? Can you put on the blinkers or something?'

'I can't move my arms,' she said.

'Why? Are they stuck or something?' he asked.

'I think they're both broken.'

'What? For real?'

'Yes. For real.'

'Oh, my God! Why didn't you say something before? You need medical attention!'

'Yes, I do.'

'Agh! I got more drips on me!' he said.

They were quiet for a while.

'Are you falling asleep?' he asked.

'Hmm?'

'Your breathing, it sounded like you were falling asleep.'

'I don't know. Yeah, maybe I was.'

'Do they hurt?'

'What?'

'Your arms.'

'Yes.'

'So ... are you going to tell my mum about this?'

She didn't answer.

'I mean, like, what are you going to tell my mum?'

'I don't know. Nothing, probably.'

'What do you mean nothing? She'll have to find out, right? She's going to flip out, isn't she?'

She didn't answer.

'Isn't she?'

'Yeah. Of course she is,' she said quietly.

'But, I mean, like ... are you going to tell her about ... you know ...'

'Listen, David. I don't know what I'm going to tell her. I'm not really going to think about that right now. So just ... leave it, okay?'

'Yeah, but – agh! The dripping is getting more! If it's petrol there might be an explosion!'

'I'm pretty sure that's just my blood.'

'What? Seriously? Oh, my God! Where are you bleeding from?'

'My head.'

'You need medical attention!'

'Yes, I do.'

There was the frantic shuffling sound again. 'I can't get my legs out! And the door won't open! Should we try yelling for help?

HELP! SOMEBODY! WE NEED HELP DOWN HERE!'
He listened to see if anyone heard him, but there was only the sound of branches scraping against the car in the wind.

'I don't think anyone can hear me,' he said.

From somewhere in the car, there was a beeping sound. The sound of a phone with a low battery.

'My phone!' he cried. 'Where is it?' More shuffling. 'It sounded like it's back here somewhere.' He grunted as he strained. 'I just can't reach behind the seat! Ugh!' He gave up in frustration.

A minute passed.

'God, I am freezing,' he said.

She didn't answer.

'Aunt Carol?'

She didn't answer.

'Aunt Carol?'

She didn't answer.

'Aunt Carol??'

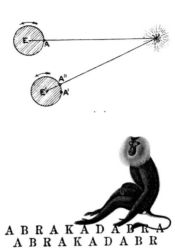

```
A B R A K A D A B R A
 A B R A K A D A B R
  A B R A K A D A B
   A B R A K A D A
    A B R A K A D
     A B R A K A
      A B R A K
       A B R A
        A B R
         A B
          A
```

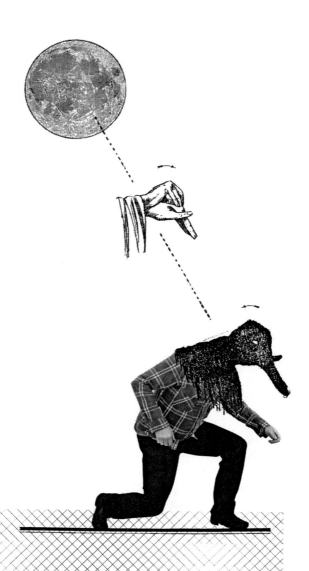

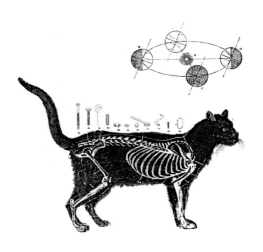

# INSTRUCTIONS

**AS INSTRUCTED,** Arthur went to the payphone outside the train station and rang the number given to him by the one-eyed tap dancer. A Russian-accented voice answered. 'Now, listen to me very carefully,' it said.

'Balthazar! Is that you?' said Arthur.

'If you ever want to see your wife alive again, you must bring the microfilms to—'

Just then a loud bus went past, drowning out Balthazar's instructions.

Balthazar was still talking. '—in room 806. Come alone, and make sure you aren't followed. You have one hour.'

'Sorry, there was a bus, I didn't catch the address,' said Arthur. But Balthazar had already hung up. 'Hello?' said Arthur. 'Hello?'

# NOVEL

**WHEN THE BISON SHUFFLED** westward that autumn, children ran out of their cabins to watch them go past. They always say the first line of a novel is important. Which makes sense, obviously. You want to grab the reader right away. And a really killer first line can make your novel famous. You know, like, 'It was the best of times, it was the worst of times,' or, 'It was a dark and stormy night,' or whatever. If you can come up with a killer first line you're fucking set, man.

Well, so I just smoked all this weed and did a line of speed and sat down to finally write a novel, and thought, 'Okay: first up I need a good first line.' And so that's what came into my head, that one about the bison. It strikes me as being rather Hemingway-esque.

I dunno. I guess it's actually kind of lame.

Well, that's okay. I'll come back and change it later. Now I'd better start getting into the story. I mean, a great first line is a good start, but really, it's all about the story. A good story is the whole point, right? Unless you want to write one of those long rambling books that are mostly about your philosophical views on the world, loosely tied together by some flimsy narrative. But I'm here to tell a good story. I'm not entirely certain what it is yet, but don't worry, I feel confident that it will pour out of me once I get going. I've got fifty-two years of life experience behind me. All these years I've been saying, 'One day I'm going to sit down and write a book, really sit down and do it,' you know? And now I'm like, 'Yes, it's time to stop *talking* about it and just fucking *do it.*' I mean, how much longer am I going to wait, right? Shit, I've known too many people who were always saying they were going to write a book and just never did. It's not just gonna happen by itself; you've got to MAKE it happen! Lock yourself in a room and fucking do it! So me, I went out and got some pot and some speed and I locked myself in this room and here we go! I feel good, I feel ready for this.

I'd better shut up about myself though and get into the story. Okay, so: we need a protagonist. Um, okay there's a guy, his name is … um … Mark. Or no, Richard. Nah, that's not really right either. Too normal, too white. Luther? Eduardo? Artie? Fred? Andreas? Neville? Idris? Fuck it, I'll call him Eric for now and change it later when I think of a better name. Okay, so: Eric. He's in his early forties and his life feels empty. Nah, fuck that, hasn't the world had enough of stories about men and their mid-life crises? I'll make him a young eager kid. Let's change his name to Will, that way I can throw some symbolism in. Free Will, strength of Will, like that. *Strength of Will* would make a pretty good title, actually. I'm going to Google that and see if it's already taken.

*

Shit. I got distracted and now two weeks have gone by and I smoked all the weed. Gotta work on this novel though, so I've got a bottle of whiskey here with me. Now, where was I up to? Oh yeah, this kid, Will. Okay. Let's say he just graduated at the top of his class from law school. Actually, on second thought, who the hell wants to read about some young lawyer? I don't know much about law anyway, I'd just be asking for trouble. Okay, let's make him a construction worker. Yeah! And he's a total bad-ass. He can out-drink and out-fight and out-fuck every other guy on his crew. But very gallant and righteous, he's always helping people out. One of those don't-judge-a-book-by-its-cover, diamond-in-the-rough kind of stories. Although now he's starting to sound rather implausible. Actually, I hate books about guys like him anyway, they make the rest of us look like assholes. Creates a standard no-one can live up to. And why does my protagonist have to be male, anyway? How about a female protagonist? Yeah! That always impresses, when a male writer can write in a convincing female voice. Might even actually get me laid after readings when I do the book tour thing. Okay, so, female protagonist. Her name is ... umm ... Cassandra. Yeah, Cassandra. She's this sultry South American babe, incredibly beautiful and with an unbelievable body. But she doesn't think she's beautiful at all, she's just really into doing pottery. She always just wears men's t-shirts with no bra. Or no – she wears worn denim overalls with nothing underneath, and leans over the wheel in her sunlight-flooded studio, her arms covered in clay, deep in concentration, dipping her hands in a bowl of water and wetting down the spinning clay, feeling the slickness as it spins under her fingers. Yeah, this is good stuff. Cassandra. And also, she has magical powers. No, no, that's going too far. I can't pull off that magical realism thing, I'm no Gabriel Garcia Marquez. Okay: beginning of story. Cassandra wakes up in the morning, stretches and rolls around in her satin sheets. She's wearing a really sexy nightgown and thin cotton underpants. She has long thick black hair and piercing blue eyes. She gets up and goes to take a shower. She slips out of the nightgown and takes off the underpants, gets under the shower. The water is warm and she luxuriates in it, sighing a deep sigh of contentment and caressing her flawless olive skin. Okay, no, wait, this is sounding like some juvenile erotic fantasy. Now that I'm thinking about it, why do the main characters in novels always have to be these unrealistic perfect people? Maybe Cassandra is just a normal looking woman. She's a bit on the chubby side, her skin isn't perfect, her hair is frizzy, she's got circles under her eyes from insomnia, she's got a pimply butt, her fingernails are chewed to nubs. But she's still really beautiful. And also very smart and nice. Everybody is nuts about her. Maybe I should change her name now, though. To Gertrude, or Bertha or something. Hmm ... nah, I like Cassandra. Okay. So Cassandra wakes up in the morning. No, wait, how about this: it starts out with Cassandra taking a shit. Hey! That's pretty original! I don't think I've ever read a novel that starts out with someone taking a shit. That should grab the reader! Okay, so.

That morning, Cassandra was sitting on the toilet, taking a shit. She stared down at her toes, wiggled them in the warmth of the blazing California sun streaming through the window. Suddenly, there was a rumble deep within the earth. Her heart leapt into her throat. Earthquake! Next thing she knew everything was moving all over the place. What an inopportune time for an earthquake! She wondered if she should run outside. But should she wipe herself first? Pull her pants up? Flush the toilet? Are you allowed to flush a toilet during an earthquake? Did she have time to wash her hands? While she fretted about all those things, the tremor subsided and all was still again. The world outside was a cacophony of car alarms.

Um. Now I'm not sure what happens. I just spent ten minutes staring at the spacebar. I'm going to go smoke a cigarette and think of ideas.

*

Fuck. Well, it's eleven months later. This novel isn't really going anywhere. Maybe I need a new approach. I always liked the kinds of books that started out with some quirky loner type guy who just goes by some weird surname, like Munston or something, travelling on a Greyhound bus one rainy night. Munston isn't right though, it's gotta be more like … Finkler? Or Barwood? Yeah, Barwood isn't bad. Okay, so this one rainy night Barwood is half asleep, half drunk on a Greyhound bus on a highway in Indiana. A crazy old Navajo woman gets on and tells him the future? Maybe he has a sexual encounter with a heroin-addicted runaway girl? Maybe he gets the shit kicked out of him by bikers. Maybe the bus stops for dinner and he somehow gets left behind. Hmm. I'm going to go smoke a cigarette and think about this.

*

Shit. I just opened this file and realised that a year and a half has passed since I wrote the above paragraph. I'm fucking fifty-five years old now. I just can't get into it. This fucking book-writing business is bullshit, anyway. Does anyone even read books any more?
You know what? Fuck this.

# THE

**THE WORD** *the* is in the dictionary. Well, alright. I suppose it has to be. But if you need to look up the word *the*, I don't see how in hell you're reading a dictionary in the first place.

# GECKO

BARRY BACKED HIS RENTAL TRUCK right up against the car park wall. Make it a bit harder to break into that way. Not that he owned anything all that flash, but still. He'd said goodbye to the two young blokes from work who'd helped him with packing, and sent them off with a case of beer by way of thanks.

When he climbed out of the truck, his neighbour was standing on the grass. She was wearing the same white sun hat she always wore. Her balloon-like shorts hung down to just above her knobbly knees.

'You moving away or something?' she said, squinting at him in the afternoon sun.

Barry was interested to hear her voice. They had never spoken, only waved to each other in passing. She looked to be about his age, or a bit younger – fifty, maybe? – but she sounded like a teenager.

'Yeah,' he replied, scratching at his beard. 'Finished up a contract here, so ... back down to Sydney.'

'Oh.' She held up a plastic grocery bag. 'I've got lychees, you want some? Or, well, what I meant is ... um ... you doing anything right now?'

Her house was a mess, she said, so they went into Barry's empty townhouse. He apologised that the only place to sit was on his bare mattress. 'I'll sleep on it one more night and then turf it out in the morning before I go,' he explained.

His neighbour's name, he learned, was Nicole. 'I always thought you looked like a nice bloke,' she told him. 'But we never stopped to talk.'

'Well, you know how it is,' said Barry.

'Yeah,' said Nicole.

*

They sat and ate lychees, making a pile of peels on the windowsill. A patch of sunlight crept across the worn carpet and started up the wall but then faded away. Meanwhile, Barry gave Nicole a cursory overview of his life thus far, and Nicole gave him a perfunctory explanation of hers. It was the usual stuff: childhood, school, marriage, job, divorce. The house, now emptied of all its contents, had already begun to reclaim the space as its own. A musty humour wafted through it. Their voices echoed strangely off the bare walls.

When it was well and truly dark, there was a lull in the conversation. Just for something to do, Barry got up and switched on the overhead light. They both groaned – it was blinding. Barry quickly turned it off again.

'I'll run next door and get some candles,' said Nicole.

She came back with candles and a bottle of wine. They drank straight from the bottle, since she hadn't brought glasses and Barry's were packed in the truck. As they passed it back and forth, she got to telling Barry about her trip to China ten years earlier, after her divorce. 'I hired a guide to take me to Hainan Island to stay among the Li people. After a few days, the chief of the tribe summoned us. He told the guide they wanted to give me a tattoo. I'd never had a tattoo or even thought about getting one, but the guide said that in all his years of taking people there nothing like that had ever happened before. He said it was a great honour and I couldn't really turn it down or else it would be insulting to them.'

Barry was fascinated by the way her eyes shone in the candlelight. He liked the way her hair fell across her shoulders. He liked the way the tip of her nose wiggled a little bit as she spoke. He liked her ankles and her feet and the chipped nail polish on her toenails. He liked the way she could go to a remote tropical island in China by herself. All this time he'd been living next door to her, completely oblivious.

'The Li women cover themselves in tattoos,' Nicole continued. 'Neck, face, arms, everywhere. It's like a coming-of-age thing. But obviously I didn't want anything that full on, so we decided I would just get a gecko. Right down here, on my hip. They're considered to be good luck, since they eat mosquitoes and mosquitoes spread malaria. They just use a really sharp thorn to prick your skin all along the outline, and then they mix soot with water and rub that into it.'

'Geez. That must have hurt.'

'Oh! Did it ever! And I was really worried about it getting infected. I was a hell of a long way from home, you know. But then this amazing thing happened that made me relax and give myself up to the moment. As I lay there getting it done, the monsoon rains came. Just like that. Whoosh.'

She was quiet then. Barry watched her pick at the dripping wax on the candles. She pursed her lips a bit and furrowed her brow, lost in thought. A strand of hair unfurled itself from behind her ear and hung straight down. When she tucked it back, she glanced up and caught Barry looking intently at her. She grinned sheepishly and looked away.

After a while she sat up and said, 'Have you left a remembrance token in this house?'

'A what?'

'Something of yours hidden away somewhere, as a symbol that you once lived here.'

'No, I haven't left anything.'

'You should!'

'Why?'

'Because! Some day, in five years or ten years, or sometime, you might be back here and you'll drive by the house – maybe you'll have people with you and you'll be showing them where you used to live, or maybe you'll be alone, I don't know – but all those years will have passed and there will be people you don't know living here, maybe the outside will be painted a different colour, and there won't be anything connecting you to the place anymore. It'll be just another house. But if you hide something away, you'll always know it's here. You'll look at the house and you'll still know something about it. You should do that with every place you live.'

Barry looked around the empty room. Then he held up the empty wine bottle. 'What about this? I could leave this.'

'That's no good. It's got to be something of yours, something that *means* something. Maybe we could look in the truck. In your boxes.'

'*This* means something. I drank it with *you*.'

She frowned and looked at him hard. 'I'm just your kooky neighbour that you never spoke to until your last day here.'

'It can still mean something.'

'Maybe.' She thought about it for a moment. 'Why is it that we never spoke before today, do you think?'

'I don't know,' said Barry. 'I sure wish we had though.'

'Maybe it's because we always thought there'd still be more time. We'd get around to it eventually. But maybe it's the opposite. We're only talking now because it's safe. You're leaving. It doesn't matter anymore. This can't turn into anything, so nobody can get hurt.'

Barry pondered this, nodding slowly.

'Or,' said Nicole quietly, 'maybe we're just the type of people that need tragedy in our lives. We need all our stories to be *what could have been*. We thrive on regret.'

After a moment, Barry said, 'I just didn't talk to you because I thought you were a weirdo.' They both laughed, but it was actually pretty much the truth.

'Funny, huh?' said Nicole. 'People like us, I mean.'

'I s'pose.'

A minute passed. Barry wasn't quite sure what to do next. Then he stood up and said, 'Right. I'm going to hide this bottle.'

Nicole clapped her hands. 'Great! Where?'

'Just up in here.' Barry pointed to the access hole in the ceiling. He looked around. 'But I've got nothing to stand on.'

'I'll hoist you up,' said Nicole. She leapt to her feet and wrapped her arms around his legs.

'That's not going to work,' said Barry. 'Let me hoist you up.' He held her tight, his arms wrapped around her legs, his face pressed against her hip as she slid the access hole cover aside and tucked the bottle away between the rafters. He liked holding her. She smelt like clean laundry and gum leaves.

'Okay, you can put me down!' she said. He staggered across the room and clumsily let her drop onto the mattress. He fell upon it beside her, breathing hard.

'I'm showing my age,' he said.

She giggled and took his hand. 'So. What next?'

He felt his ears turn red. He swallowed, then cleared his throat and said, 'Could I see the gecko?'

\*

Clouds hung low over the Pacific Highway. Barry drove through the rain for hours, mesmerised by the whir and swish of the windscreen wipers, the hiss of tyres on wet road, and the soft background babble of news radio. The whole world was awash. Barry felt strange. It had been a long time since he'd stayed up all night.

But there was something else to it. He couldn't stop thinking about Nicole. It made a lump in his throat. His mind burned with her bare skin, the feel of her, of the scent of her. And every kilometre he drove took him further away. What was he doing? What was waiting for him in Sydney? He came very close several times to turning around and going back. Just like in the movies. He could turn up soaking wet at her house with a bouquet of flowers, sing her a song, propose to her on one knee. But wasn't he too old for such silly thoughts?

He finally pulled off the highway in Port Macquarie and got out his phone. Somewhere back up there in Lismore, her phone rang.

And she answered.

He had so many things he wanted to tell her, all jumbled in his brain, trying to get out. She'd changed him, opened him up. He wanted to know her, have her be part of his life, share all his thoughts with her. He wanted her to know how lost he'd felt until he'd met her. He wished she was experiencing this rainy drive with him, he'd love to hear what she had to say about it. He wanted so badly to have her there, to find a motel, crawl between crisp clean sheets with her, see the gecko again.

But all he could say was, 'How are you?'

She was tired but good, she said. She'd slept for a couple of hours after he'd gone but then had woken up and couldn't get back to sleep. Yes, it was raining there too. She was just pottering around the house a bit, probably go to the shops later on.

He had a million questions. What was she thinking? What was she feeling? What was she doing later? What was she doing the next day? What was she wearing? But it felt awkward to ask. He said he missed her. She said she missed him too. He really wanted to say I love you, but that seemed a bit crazy. So he said he'd call her from Sydney.

But then one thing led to another and he never did.

# SHADY OAKS

**THE VERY OLD MAN** slowly made his way down the hallway. He began each step by carefully nudging his walker a short distance ahead of him; he then slid his right foot forward and gradually transferred his weight onto the walker's frame, then pulled his left foot in under him and shifted his weight back onto it.

In this laborious manner, he proceeded past a succession of open doors, the engraved plastic nameplates on the wall beside them identifying the residents of each room. Crystal. Brittany. Brandon. Josh. Zack. Courtney. Tiffany. Brent. Nick. Danielle.

At last he reached his destination: Chad.

He manoeuvred his way into Chad's room, and found Chad sitting on his bed, staring vacantly out the window. Chad only had a few wisps of snow white hair left atop his spotted head, and it stuck out rather comically in all directions. Wrinkled flesh hung from his bony arms, a mass of discoloured skin all that remained of what had once been some pretty badass Japanese warrior sleeve tatts.

'Yo, man, what up?' said the very old man from the doorway, then had a brief but intense coughing fit.

Chad, startled out of his reverie, turned to stare at his visitor, his jaw slack as he blinked in confusion for a moment. Then he grinned.

'Hey, Kyle dude,' he said in a raspy voice. 'What's happening?'

Kyle made his way to the armchair beside Chad's bed, slid his walker to one side, and very carefully lowered himself down. 'Just saw on Facebook,' he said. 'Another one of my homies ate it. This guy Evan. Played drums in a couple bands I was in.'

'Shit, bro, that's lame. Sorry to hear that,' said Chad. He adjusted the oxygen tube in his nose.

Kyle absent-mindedly fingered the long dangling loop of flesh that hung from his earlobe, a remnant from where his ear gauge had once been. 'Like probably more than half my Facebook friends are dead, man,' he said. 'It's fuckin' weird.'

'Well, Facebook is for old people,' said Chad. 'Ask any of the nurses here if they're on Facebook. They'll laugh at you.'

'True dat. You seen the dinner menu yet?' asked Kyle.

'Yeah. Chicken Cordon Bleu.'

'Oh, sweet.'

A rhythmic clunking sound from the hallway had been getting steadily louder, and now a tiny, stooped woman with a quad cane appeared in the doorway. Her bright-red lipstick stood in stark contrast to the almost translucent skin of her face. She waved a liver-spotted hand. 'Hey, homos,' she croaked.

'Amber!' said Chad. 'Wassup, beeatch?'

Kyle twisted himself around in the armchair. 'Back from Saint John's,' he said. 'How's the new knee?'

'Well, I'm walking, right?' said Amber. She worked her jaw wildly for a moment. Damn dentures.

'Come here, sit down,' said Chad, moving his legs aside to make some room on the bed.

'Well aren't you the gentleman,' said Amber. She crossed to the bed, then, with great care, got herself seated. Her cargo pants slid off her skeletal hips enough to reveal a faded and blurry tattoo of a butterfly surrounded by scrolls and flowers on her lower back – a tramp stamp, they used to call it – just above her adult diaper.

'Dude, the food in that hospital sucks ass,' she said.

'Chicken Cordon Bleu here tonight,' said Kyle.

'Sweet,' said Amber. 'So what's been happening while I've been gone?'

'Not much,' said Chad. 'Well, actually, Danny had a stroke.'

'Shit. He okay?'

'Nah. He's pretty fucked up.'

'Oh, lame. I should go visit him.'

'Yeah.'

'Hey, I saw this cool thing in the news,' said Kyle. 'They've restored an old McDonald's. A little freestanding building, like they used to be, remember? Somehow there was an old abandoned one still left, out in the burbs somewhere. And so now they've fixed it up. We should go check it out.'

'Cool. Do they serve food?' asked Chad.

'Nah, it's just a museum. The Historical Society did it.'

'Pfff. What's the point then?'

A cheerful young Indian nurse barrelled into the room pushing a trolley. 'Oh!' she exclaimed. 'The gang's all here!'

'Hey, Grace,' said Chad, Kyle and Amber.

'How's everyone doing this morning?' asked Grace.

'Pretty good,' said Amber.

'Fine,' said Kyle.

'Fantastic!' said Grace. 'Hey, so are any of you guys going to the lunchtime concert today?'

'I dunno,' said Kyle. 'What's on?'

'Well, we've got a band coming that will be playing that old-time music that you like,' said Grace. 'The grunge, and metal, and that sort of thing. In the Lilac Room at eleven-thirty.'

Amber, Kyle and Chad looked at each other enquiringly, and then all nodded slightly.

'Yeah, that could be cool,' said Chad.

'Yeah, we might go,' said Amber.

Grace examined the labels on some containers and doled out Chad, Kyle and Amber's medication. They all swallowed the pills. Grace went to the window. 'Nice out today,' she remarked.

Chad rolled his eyes. 'It's never *nice* out anymore,' he said. 'You do know that the sky used to be blue, right?'

'Yes,' said Grace, 'of course. But a yellow sky is all I've ever known. So to me, it's a nice day.'

'It was nicer with a blue sky,' said Chad.

Annoyance flickered across Grace's face, then she brightened up again. 'Okay, I'll be back later this morning to check on you,' she said, and pushed her trolley back out the door.

'God, she's a cunt,' said Chad when Grace was out of earshot.

'What's your fucking problem with her?' asked Amber. 'She's a sweetie.'

'She's such a phony.'

'Well, what do you expect? Dealing with us old fucks all day.'

'She's actually kind of hot,' said Kyle. 'I'd totally do her.'

Amber and Chad laughed.

'Alright, well, I'm going to go visit poor Danny,' said Amber, and began getting to her feet.

'I'll come with,' said Kyle, and started pulling himself up out of his armchair. 'You coming, bro?'

'Nah,' said Chad. 'Guy's a vegetable. He won't even know you're there. What's the point?'

'Dude, what is *up* with you?' asked Amber.

'I dunno, man. I'm just sick of sitting around waiting to die. What's the fucking point, you know? This shit sucks donkey dicks.'

'Well, yeah, it does,' said Amber. 'But what else are you gonna do?'

'Come on,' said Kyle. 'Get your ass off that bed and let's go do something.'

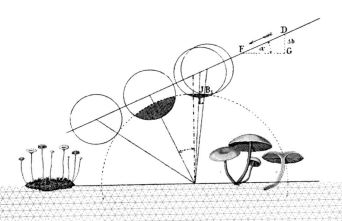

# THE LAST WILKIE'S

**BY THE TIME SHE GOT TO** Ocelot Springs, Erin's hands ached from clenching the steering wheel. The last hour of driving had been harrowing, all fog and sporadic downpours, the road's condition worsening as it wound its way up into the gloomy hills. It was only just after midday, but it felt like dusk was already settling in. The air carried a wet chill. Even the trees looked hostile.

The town itself, Ocelot Springs, was a real backwater. Erin drove right through it from one end to the other, trying in vain to find a street name or building number. A couple of haggard locals gawked at her as she cruised by, or maybe it was the shiny rental car that was drawing their attention. The few other cars Erin saw were older than hers by a couple of decades. Bits of trash drifted around in the street. None of the shops were open and Erin couldn't really tell what they'd be selling if they were. No chain stores or anything, not even a proper petrol station. At one point she had to brake hard when a pack of dogs swarmed across the road.

And then she was out the other end of town and back in the dark woods. Had she missed it? Must have done. She was looking for a safe place to turn around when she spotted the familiar blue and yellow sign up ahead: *Wilkie's*. But to her astonishment, the sign was *on*. Aglow. Lit up like a beacon shining through the gloom. As she got closer, she could see lights on inside the restaurant. There was a car parked out front. She could see people inside. Customers at a table, eating. Someone in a Wilkie's uniform was cleaning the windows.

The place was open for business.

Her heart pounding, Erin drove slowly past. A hundred metres down the road she pulled over and switched off the engine. She sat there, with no idea what to do next. The place was *open*! How was that *possible*?

Her first solo trip and already she was going to have to call Gary for help. This job was supposed to be a piece of cake, just a straight inventory and assessment of saleable assets and then back out of town before the sun went down. Back at her hotel with a bottle of wine and some takeaway in time for the seven o'clock news. She so badly wanted to prove that she was just as capable as any of the others. But this – this was a situation unheard of. What would the others do?

Given that the Wilkie's Family Restaurant Corporation had ceased to be an entity in any way, shape or form some ten months previously, it was quite extraordinary to find this one still fully operational. But did she have any authority to shut it down? Even if she did, who was going to listen to her? Who did have the authority? Should she summon the police? Were there even police in Ocelot Springs? She supposed she should speak to the people running the place. But what was she meant to tell them, exactly? Erin had absolutely no idea, so she fished her phone out of the briefcase she'd bought specially for this trip and tried to ring the office. But there was no reception, which was not exactly a surprise.

She twisted around to look back at the restaurant, and spotted a payphone along its side wall. A *payphone*! Who has those anymore? She slipped out of the car and into the drizzle, then hurried back up the road like a commando, approaching from the flank to secure the phone. To her great relief, there was a dial tone. She followed the instructions to make a reverse charge call. Linda answered, accepted the charges, and put her through to Gary.

'Erin!' He guffawed. 'You find the place okay? What's with the reverse charge? You lose your phone again? So. Talk to me. What have we got? Anything worth a damn?'

She cupped her hand over the mouthpiece and spoke softly. 'Gary, the place is still open.'

'Oh, yeah, that happens sometimes. Don't worry about it. Franchisee's supposed to secure the door when they leave, but they forget, or don't care.'

'No! I mean it's open for business. Lights on, people inside.'

'Oh! Must be some locals using it as a community hangout or something. They're trespassing on private property. You're going to need to call the sheriff's office and get a bailiff out there. Just show them the papers.'

'No, Gary, it's operating as a *Wilkie's*. People are eating in there. Employees in blue and yellow uniforms are working. The sign is all lit up.'

'What? But I don't – how could they – that's just not – I can't…'

Erin had never heard Gary flustered before. In a strange sort of way, it made her giddy with delight.

'So wait,' he finally said, 'where are you now?'

'I'm right outside! I'm on a payphone right in the fucking car park!'

'And you're sure you're at the right place?'

She clenched her fist around the receiver. 'Of course it's the right place. What the fuck? Do you think I'm a complete idiot or something?'

'Well so have you gone inside and talked to anyone?'

'No! I don't know what the hell I'm supposed to say. That's why I'm calling you. What do I tell them?'

'Tell them they're not supposed to be there! They're going to have to shut down right away. They've got no liability insurance! What if someone gets injured? We could be in some serious shit!'

'But why would they listen to me? If I walk in and say you've got to get out of here, they're not just going to say oh, okay, and go, are they? I feel like I'm going to need some backup here. I'm not sure I'd trust the cops around here, though. I don't even know if this town has any cops.'

'Erin, listen to me. They don't own the place anymore, we do. Okay? The fridges, fryers, grill, the seats and tables, the ground it's on, whatever that's worth, it's all ours now. We're just doing our job here. Have confidence in your authority. You've got the files with you, right? Look up the franchise holder's name—'

'Yeah, I did already; it's Daniel Corby.'

'Great, okay, so just go in there and find the guy, tell him the deal. Wilkie's is no more. I mean, does he not *know* that? We sent him letters! He must have gotten the letters! Ask him why he never responded. Tell him it was assumed that he'd abandoned the place, that's why we've left it so long. That and its remote location. Jesus. I don't even know how he's managed to keep it running, but he's got to close right away. And then do your inventory and report back. We need to close the books on Wilkie's before the end of the financial year.'

She sighed and closed her eyes. 'This is fucked up, Gary. This was supposed to be an easy one.'

Gary put on his patronising voice. 'Yes, Erin, I understand that this is an unexpected turn of events. But you have been assuring me for quite some time that you're ready to step into the role of field assessor, and that requires an ability to think laterally, to demonstrate initiative, and to adapt to changing situations on the ground.'

Erin picked at the deteriorating rubber seal around the payphone's glass. 'There's something really creepy about this place. I don't feel very comfortable with this whole scenario.'

'Well, I don't really know what alternatives we have at this point, Erin. I don't think it would make sense to just have you come back home and then book someone more senior to go out there and deal with the situation. I'd lose a lot of time and money that way. Can you at least just go talk to the guy? Don't make your trip a complete waste. They're not going to kill you and chop you up and turn you into burgers, for Chrissake!'

'Alright, fine. Fuck. Fine. I'll talk to them.'

Erin hung up, took a deep breath, then walked around to the front and entered the restaurant.

Two old men sat at a table, eating burgers and fries. A young girl in uniform was going from table to table refilling napkin dispensers while a young man, also in uniform, was putting a fresh bin liner into a bin. The place was clean and well lit and the walls still bore the placards advertising the special limited-time-only offers from ten months earlier. Free *Captain Slamdunk* cup with the purchase of any value meal. That film had long since come and gone from theatres. It was like the place was frozen in time, preserved at the moment of the franchise's demise. Erin had visited dozens of Wilkie's around that time, and it was a surreal trip down memory lane to be back in an operational one now. She looked up at the menu and noticed that some alterations had been made: several items were covered over with electrical tape, and some new non-standard Wilkie's items had been added. Where new words and letters were needed they had been carefully crafted by hand to match the existing ones.

Upon Erin's entrance, the girl had set aside the napkin dispensers and gone around behind the counter. She beamed brightly. 'Welcome to Wilkie's! May I take your order?'

Startled, Erin froze, and then stammered, 'Um ... yes. I'll have a Little Wilkie's meal.' Her usual order. The words just came automatically.

'Certainly! And to drink?'

'Um ... a Diet Coke, please.'

'Would you like to upsize your meal for only an additional forty cents?'

'Thanks, no, that's fine.'

'Can I interest you in an ice-cream sundae this afternoon?'

'No, thank you.'

The girl rang up the sale. 'Your total today is six dollars and sixty cents.'

Erin fished a ten out of her bag and handed it over. Through the burger chute behind the girl, she could see that the young man who'd been putting in the bin liner was back in the kitchen, watching for the order to come up on his video monitor. He now went into action, disappearing from view. The girl gave Erin her change and said, 'Go on and take a seat, ma'am, I'll bring it out to your table.'

Erin went and sat by the window. The two old men stared at her unabashedly, chewing their food. She pulled the Wilkie's file out of her briefcase and flipped through until she found the dossier on the franchise holder. Name: Daniel Corby. Age: 56. It didn't have much more to say about him, other than that in 1993 he had attended the requisite six-week training and induction required for all Wilkie's franchise holders worldwide. The Ocelot Springs Wilkie's had opened the following year. This was his only Wilkie's.

She stared out the window into the gloomy wet afternoon. She didn't know how to tackle this situation. She was really more of a research and support person, spreadsheets and presentations. But fieldwork had seemed so glamorous. Flying Business Class, staying in hotels, driving rental cars, wearing a suit. Carrying a briefcase. She'd pestered Gary incessantly to let her tag along with other field assessors, and finally to go on her own. And now here she was, way out of her depth. Why had she ordered food? Why not just ask to speak to Daniel Corby? To buy some time, perhaps? What was that going to accomplish? The truth was, she'd panicked.

Several minutes had passed. She craned her neck towards the counter and noticed that the girl was cutting larger napkins down to size with scissors and stamping the trademark 'W' on them with a rubber stamp. The girl glanced up and caught Erin watching her. 'Shouldn't be much longer,' she chirped. 'Thanks for your patience!' A burger and a container of fries slid down the chute and a bell rang. The girl placed them on a tray that already had a Diet Coke on it, then brought the tray over to Erin's table and set it before her. 'Here you are, ma'am. Can I get you anything else?'

'Uh, no, thanks.' Erin examined the items before her. Her Diet Coke was indeed in a *Captain Slamdunk* cup as advertised, but it was a just a cheap plastic orange cup onto which the *Captain Slamdunk* character had been carefully drawn by hand with a Sharpie. Her burger was in a box that seemed to have been made from a manila folder, cut down and assembled with sticky tape, stamped with the same W logo. The fries appeared to be hand-cut potatoes, and were served in a sleeve constructed from a paper towel tube. Everything was served on a photocopied tray liner. *Help Wilkie save Lady Pickles from the Munchkins by connecting the dots.* Erin took a small, cautious bite of the burger. It tasted peculiar. She put it down, sighed heavily, then got up and approached the counter.

The girl looked concerned. 'Is your meal alright, ma'am?'

'Is Daniel Corby around? Can I see him?'

The girl froze, her eyes wide. 'I'm sorry, he's not here at the moment. Can I ask what it's in reference to?'

'Do you know how I can contact him?'

Without taking her eyes off Erin, the girl shouted, 'Victor!'

From the back came the young man's voice. 'What?' When the girl didn't reply, he came up the passageway to the front, looking concerned. 'What is it?'

'This lady wants to talk to Dan.'

Victor shot the girl an angry look, then turned to Erin. 'What do you want with Dan?'

His aggressive tone was unsettling. Her heart thundered in her chest. She tried to think how Gary would handle this situation. He would probably cock a cheeky eyebrow and keep a twinkle in his eye, but go for the throat. She tried to form her mouth into a confident smirk. 'I have some business to discuss with him. Of a confidential nature.'

'Well, he's not here. Don't know when he will be. He's not around much.'

'Can you give me a number where I can reach him?'

'No. He's not interested in any business of yours. You should just leave.' He took the girl's hand and led her down the passageway to the back. Erin could hear agitated whispering, then nothing. She waited a few minutes but they didn't reappear. She peered through the food chute to the back but couldn't see anyone, so finally she just gathered up the Wilkie's dossier and her briefcase and went back to her car.

She sat with her hands on the steering wheel, staring at the back of the restaurant in the rear view mirror. How was she supposed to talk to Corby if she couldn't find him? Maybe he was even in there right now, holed up in an office in back somewhere. So what was she supposed to do next? She thought about calling Gary again but knew he would just make her feel stupid. He always had all the answers, he always knew just what to say and do. So what would he do if he were here? She tried to picture him in the restaurant. His fat gut, his loud tie, waving his meaty finger in that Victor kid's face. He would probably just push his way behind the counter like he owned the place, which technically he actually did, and go looking for Corby. Erin couldn't imagine herself doing that in a million years.

As she sat there, an old utility truck came rattling past her down the road and veered in to park at the back of the building. A man in a raincoat climbed out and opened the tailgate, then stood examining the contents. Victor erupted from the back door of the restaurant and spoke animatedly to the man, pointing at Erin's car. The girl came out as well, and stood anxiously wringing her hands. The raincoat man listened to Victor, throwing a couple of glances Erin's way. Must be Corby, thought Erin. She summoned all her courage and got out of the car.

As she crossed the road, Victor became frantic. 'That's her! That's her!'

'Victor, calm yourself, please,' said the man.

Erin stopped a few metres away from them. 'Mr Corby,' she said. Her voice sounded high and fluty. She tried again, lower and more authoritative. 'Mr Corby. I'd like a word with you, please.'

Corby didn't acknowledge her. 'Victor,' he said, 'I have obtained some meat. Would you please carry it inside and prep it for the dinner rush. Cathy, there are a couple of bags on the passenger seat containing cardboard. Take them inside and see what you can do with them. Also, I believe I found a coil we can use to fix the ice machine.' His gaze briefly swept over Erin and then back to Victor. 'Where is Nino?'

'Hasn't been in yet today,' said Victor.

'Alright, that's fine then. Now, both of you please do as I asked.'

As Victor and Cathy retrieved their respective parcels from the truck, Corby took a small piece of wire out of his pocket and examined it.

Victor, a large canvas sack slung over his shoulder, paused on his way back into the restaurant and looked anxiously at Corby, who, with only the briefest of gestures, waved him along. Cathy followed quickly behind him.

Corby replaced the wire in his pocket and looked at his watch. 'Hmm,' he said to no-one in particular, stroking his moustache and gazing off down the road. 'Nino.'

'Mr Corby,' said Erin again.

At last he brought his gaze around and fixed it upon her. He had strange blue eyes that made Erin jittery. She waited for him to speak, but after several seconds he only nodded politely, then walked quickly into the restaurant and pulled the door shut behind him.

'Hey!' Erin ran to the door but found it locked. She pounded on it. 'Mr Corby!' She felt like an idiot. Who was she kidding? She'd wanted so badly to be more than just an office worker, but it was obvious she was way out of her depth. She trudged over to the payphone and picked up the handset. What was she going to tell Gary this time? What was he going to say? She couldn't face it. She briefly entertained the idea of just getting in the car and driving away. In two and a half hours she could be back in her hotel room, sinking into a blissful hot bath. Wine. Takeaway. Television. But then she thought of having to explain that to Gary. *You found the guy, and then you just left!*

So she slammed the handset back down, walked around to the front of the building and went inside.

Corby was standing behind the counter. With his raincoat off, she could see that he was well-groomed, wearing a pale yellow polo shirt, and had a name tag that said 'DAN' and beneath that, 'Manager'. As she approached, a huge grin spread across his face. His strange eyes twinkled.

'Welcome to Wilkie's, home of the quality family dining experience,' he said. 'May I take your order?'

'I'm Erin MacMillan from Williamson and Farmer, Mr Corby,' she said. 'As you may be aware, we are an administration and insolvency firm. We have made numerous attempts to contact you regarding—'

'Yes, Wilkie's is committed to providing quality food at a price that families can afford. Just look for the blue and yellow W, and you know you will get great food, great service and great value.' The smile remained in place.

'Sir, please, I need you to listen to me. I don't know how you have managed to keep this place running without any support or supplies from corporate headquarters, but I'm sure you are aware that the Wilkie's Foodservice Group has filed for bankruptcy and gone into liquidation. I mean … you know that, right?'

'Can I interest you in a Wilkie's Meal today, ma'am? It comes with a free *Captain Slamdunk* cup!'

'I'm sorry, Mr Corby, but your restaurant is going to have to close down. Uh, effective immediately. This building and everything in it are now the property of Williamson and Farmer and our obligation to the creditors is to liquidate all assets and distribute the proceeds. There's also the matter of operating without liability insurance.'

Corby blinked a few times. His eyes drifted to the windows at the front of the store, looking expectantly outside, then back to Erin again. His smile slowly ebbed. He sniffed and cleared his throat.

Erin tried again. 'Mr Corby?'

'Come this way,' he said finally. 'Let's talk in my office.'

Erin went around behind the counter and followed him down the passageway to the back. The walls were covered with motivational posters, reminding employees that customers were the top priority and service should always come with a smile. As they crossed the large prep room, she had a brief opportunity to look over what equipment there was. She saw things held together by duct tape and wire, odds and ends not standard to the Wilkie's kitchen fit-out.

'This way, please,' said Corby and motioned her into a small office. He sat down at the desk and pushed some papers off a chair to make a place for her. The shelves were stacked with file folders and binders. There was a large poster mounted directly over the desk. It showed a lion in mid-stride, chasing a gazelle. The text read, *Every morning the gazelle knows it has to outrun the fastest lion in order to survive. Every morning the lion knows it has to outrun the slowest gazelle in order to survive. Whether you're a lion or a gazelle – when you wake up, you'd better hit the ground running.*

Erin cleared her throat and placed her briefcase in her lap. She tried to think how Gary would handle himself in this situation. Very professional, but a bit intimidating. She took a stern tone. 'Now, Mr Corby,' she began. 'Did you not receive any of the letters sent to you by my firm? Is your telephone no longer connected? Numerous attempts have been made to contact you. I have to wonder why you neglected to respond and continued to run your store when surely you must have been aware that the company had gone into receivership.' Her heart was beating rapidly and she was trembling a bit. What made it worse was that Corby obviously could see how nervous she was, and planned to exploit her weakness. His eyes narrowed and he smiled slyly.

'Ms MacMillan,' he said, 'Wilkie's is more than just a corporation. It's a mindset. It's a way of life. It transcends matters of money and corporate law.'

'If you wanted to keep your restaurant open you could have purchased it at a very fair price, changed the name and run it independently. That was clearly outlined in our letters to you. Plenty of franchise owners did just that. But there are procedures to be followed. Cutting off communication and becoming essentially a renegade branch of Wilkie's is not … it's just … well … it's not acceptable. And kind of crazy, actually.'

'Ah. So you think I'm crazy.'

'I don't know you, Mr Corby. It's not my place to make that judgment. But it seems to me rather unprofessional to ignore business correspondence and flout the proper procedures.'

Corby drew himself up indignantly. 'I have been nothing but exemplary in my professionalism since the day I opened this restaurant. My establishment has been a model for others to follow. We have consistently achieved very high customer approval ratings, and have received no fewer than fourteen commendations of merit from corporate headquarters. Ms MacMillan, when I attended the orientation program at Wilkie's corporate headquarters prior to opening this restaurant, I took the lessons I learned there to heart. I came to understand that Wilkie's is more than just a business; it is a way of being. It doesn't end when our work hours are over. By being Wilkie's people all the time, we make it a Wilkie's world. I have applied the Wilkie's principles I learned there to the best of my ability every single day since. If others have now chosen to turn their backs on Wilkie's, that is their choice. But not a choice I am prepared to make.'

'It's not a question of choice! It's over, Mr Corby. Wilkie's is gone.'

'It's not gone, Ms MacMillan. This is Wilkie's right here. You are sitting in Wilkie's right this very moment, are you not?'

'You've lost touch with reality! Look around you. This place is barely operational. It's held together by duct tape! You're running a ten-month-old promotion! *Captain Slamdunk* isn't playing in theatres anymore! It's ancient history. *Captain Slamdunk 2* is about to come out.'

Corby looked over Erin's shoulder and smiled. 'Nino! It's about time.'

Erin turned around. A large man was standing in the doorway. A very large man.

'Sorry I'm late, boss,' said Nino. 'I got these.' He held up three dead rabbits. Blood dripped softly on the floor. Erin remembered the peculiar taste of the bite of burger she'd taken and her stomach heaved.

'Very good, Nino. Just leave them on the prep table. Victor will take care of them. I have something I need you to do.' He levelled his gaze at Erin. 'Would you excuse me for a moment?'

Corby sidled past Erin out of the office and pulled Nino into a storage room where they began a hushed conversation.

Erin tried to calculate her chances of making it to the front of the restaurant and out the door before they could catch her. But even if she got out the door, she wouldn't necessarily be home free. She'd need to get to her car. If she could get out the back door she'd have a better chance, but she wasn't sure where it was. Would they even give chase? Was she actually in danger or was she being completely paranoid? Maybe she could just walk out. But then how would she explain to Gary that she'd been in the back of the store, talking to Corby in his office, and then had just left?

She stood up and took a few steps out of the office, into the prep room, and was finally able to have a good look around. They were using what looked like a gear box from an old car mounted on an engine lift as an industrial mixer. The grill was clearly not in use, as it was piled with cardboard boxes; a regular backyard barbecue stood in front of it, presumably where Victor had cooked her rabbit burger earlier. Mounted to the prep table was an old-fashioned, hand-cranked meat mincer. Definitely not standard issue Wilkie's equipment – the franchisees had received burgers pre-formed and frozen, delivered weekly to all franchisees by big Wilkie's trucks. Boxes and canned goods were stacked on a large metal shelving unit along one wall. Not the big industrial-sized cans with the 'W' logo that came in the deliveries, but regular-sized cans from the grocery store. Chopped tomatoes, pickles, sliced beetroot, sliced pineapple. On a tall shelf were stacks of empty burger boxes waiting to have burgers put in them. They were all irregular – hand-made with sticky tape, and with the 'W' stamped on them. The industrial fridge and freezer stood against the back wall, bits of duct tape evident in places. Erin had to admit some degree of respect for these people. It must have taken immense resourcefulness and ingenuity to keep the place running semi-normally all this time. It couldn't have been easy.

A door slammed somewhere and Victor stomped into the prep room. He stopped abruptly when he saw Erin, then stared at her but said nothing as he put on a butcher's apron and took a large cleaver off a hook. He began hacking at the rabbit carcasses, stripping off the skin and then pulling muscle off bone and stuffing the bits of flesh into the top of the meat mincer.

Erin began slowly moving towards the passageway that led up to the front of the restaurant. She wondered where Cathy was, and whether she would prove to be friend or foe if it came down to it. She watched Victor carefully, but he was absorbed in his work. She made estimates of the number of steps down the short hallway, around the service counter, across the dining room and out the door. She inched closer to the corridor, every muscle tensed and ready to make a run for it.

Then Corby and Nino emerged abruptly from the storage room, prompting Erin to make a frantic dash. But her business shoes found no traction on the greasy floor and she skidded madly into the large shelving unit. She grabbed on to it but it tipped forward under her weight, dumping her heavily onto the floor. She wrenched her shoulder and felt a sharp pain on her shin as it collided with the lowest shelf. Cans, boxes and heavy mixing bowls cascaded off the shelves onto her head and shoulders. She writhed madly in confusion, pain and panic on the slimy tiles. Then a pair of large meaty hands took hold of her and hoisted her to her feet.

Up close, Nino had an earthy smell, like a forest floor. Pain seared through her body – shoulder, knee, head, foot. She tried desperately to twist out of his grip, kicking at him, which only made him hold her more securely. 'Hold *still*,' he said. After a while, all the fight drained out of her. She hung limply in his hands, exhausted and resigned.

'Bring her to the office,' said Corby.

Nino hustled her into the office and put her in the desk chair. He wrenched open a large desk drawer and pulled out a first aid kit. As she stared at the poster of the lion and gazelle, he dabbed at the cuts on her head and legs with cotton balls, then bandaged the gash on her shin. 'Got to be careful in a food-service environment,' he told her as he worked. 'Walk, don't run. Think before you act. Safety first. Accident prevention is your number one intention. Wash your hands before returning to work.'

Corby came in and handed her one of the hand-drawn *Captain Slamdunk* cups. 'Thought you might be thirsty.' She took it and guzzled it down before even considering what it might be. She peered into the empty cup suspiciously as she pondered the taste. It was Diet Coke. It did make her feel better.

'I'm afraid we're going to have to leave you on your own now,' said Corby. 'The dinner rush is about to hit us and I'm going to need all hands on deck for a couple of hours.'

'Dinner rush,' said Erin vaguely.

'The sawmill lets out at five,' Corby explained.

And so Erin was left on her own in the office. She sat there for half an hour in a semi-stupor, staring at the lion and thinking, what would Gary do now? She became aware of an increasing din coming from the front of the store. It sounded busy. She wanted to see this. She got to her feet and limped out of the office. Victor was at the barbecue, furiously cooking burgers, while Nino sliced potatoes into fries and threw them in handfuls into the fryers, then prepared buns in boxes lined up on the table. Neither noticed her as she slipped past and hobbled up the corridor.

She peered around the corner and saw Corby at the counter, taking orders. There was a long line of rough-looking men, tired and grubby. Some women and children sat at tables. The place was packed. Corby radiated cheerful energy, grinning his bright grin as he took each order, greeting his customers by name. Cathy scurried around behind him, fetching drinks and putting food on trays as Victor slid burgers and fries down the chute from the back.

A man with a scraggly beard and a couple of teeth missing reached the head of the queue. 'Things are a bit tight this week, Dan,' he said sheepishly. 'I was laid up sick for a couple of days. Can you float us tonight and I'll square it next week?'

Corby held up a hand. 'Of course, Walter, that's no problem at all. Are Suzie and the boys dining with you today?' Corby looked around the dining area, spotted a woman and two young boys at a table, and waved. They waved back. 'So that'll be the Wilkie's Family Combo Deal?' Walter nodded. Corby punched the order into the register.

Next in line was a father and son. 'Big Wilkie's Deluxe Meal for me,' said the father, 'and a Junior Wilkie's Meal for Tommy.'

'Does it still come with a *Captain Slamdunk* cup?' asked the boy.

'Certainly does!' said Corby. He leaned in conspiratorially and lowered his voice. 'Which character are you missing from your collection?'

The boy thought for a moment, placing a finger on his lips. 'Umm...' He held up the finger. 'I still need Starla.'

Corby nodded. He hunted through the cups under the counter for a moment, then called Cathy over and whispered something to her. Cathy nodded and hurried towards the back. She was startled to encounter Erin as she rushed past into the corridor. She froze for a moment, not sure what to do, but then continued to the back. Erin followed her, limping back down the corridor.

Cathy was hurriedly drawing a figure on a cup with a Sharpie. As Erin approached, she explained, 'We ran out of Starlas.' She held up the cup to show a shaky drawing of a woman with an hourglass figure spinning a basketball on her finger. 'Not bad, right?'

'So many customers,' said Erin. 'Is this usual?'

'On weeknights, yeah,' said Cathy. 'Used to be even busier, when the copper mine was still open.' She glanced towards the front briefly. 'Can I show you something?' she asked.

'Sure,' said Erin. 'What?'

'Just a second!'

Cathy ran to the office. There was the sound of a drawer slamming and she ran back holding a framed photograph. It showed the Ocelot Springs Wilkie's with a full complement of staff standing out front, all in brand new uniforms.

Erin took the photograph into her hands and stared at it. Corby stood proudly at the front of the group, looking much younger. Victor stood beside him, sticking out his tongue and making a peace sign. Cathy pointed to a wispy teenager at the back. 'There's me,' she said. 'This was the day we opened. Dan was a minister before, you know. But his church had to close.'

From out front, Corby shouted, '*Cathy! Need you up here!*'

'Got to get back,' said Cathy. She hurried back up the corridor with the cup.

Victor and Nino were hard at work. Victor was scooping minced meat out of a plastic tub, forming it into patties and throwing them on the barbecue as fast as he could, then flipping the ones he had on the go. A row of the hand-made burger boxes was lined up on the prep table, each with half a bun in it. Nino pulled peeled potatoes out of a tub of water and sliced them expertly into fries. As Erin watched, he pulled up a fryer, dumped out its contents and salted them, then began scooping them into homemade cartons and sending them through the food chute to the front.

Erin leaned heavily against the wall. All she wanted now was quiet. To lie down, to slip into the oblivion of sleep. Victor noticed her wobbling. 'You okay?' he called over. She nodded. She hobbled into the office, put the photograph on the desk and picked up her briefcase. She found the back door and pushed her way out. It was pouring rain and only the faintest hint of light was left in the sky. She reached her car, got in, brushed the wet hair out of her eyes. Found the keys, started the engine, turned around and drove back in the direction of Ocelot Springs. The Wilkie's car park was full. The place looked cheerful. Warm and well-lit amid the dark, foreboding trees.

As she drove back through Ocelot Springs, she saw no signs of life. No lights were on, nobody was out, she didn't pass a single other car.

An interminable two and a half hours later, she stumbled up to the door of her hotel room. There was a message from reception taped to it. *Anticipating update ASAP on status of Ocelot Springs.* She pulled her phone out of her briefcase and checked it. Ten missed calls. She could picture Gary drumming his fat fingers impatiently, the way he always did when the world failed to meet his expectations. She pulled the note down, opened the door, flung her briefcase onto one bed and sprawled onto the other.

She lay there, savouring the quiet. The only sound was the distant growl every now and then of a semi-trailer roaring past out on the highway. She tried to make sense of the day, though her brain was too exhausted to think straight. There was something admirable about Corby and his gang, the way they managed to keep that Wilkie's running. She couldn't see how they could do it much longer, though. It had to end eventually. But that town was nearly dead; the Wilkie's was the only thing it had going for it. But then was it her place to try to save some hillbilly mountain town? What was she supposed to do now? Could she live with being responsible for shutting down the only restaurant in Ocelot Springs? What would become of Corby? What would become of Victor, and Nino, and poor Cathy? She thought about flying home the next day, going in to the office and quitting. How satisfying it would be to see Gary's face! But then what would she do? She had mortgage payments to make. And that Wilkie's was going to get shut down anyway, whether she was part of the process or not. And surely Corby knew that it had to end sooner or later. But it just didn't sit right with her for loud, fat Gary to come out on top, as he always did, while Corby and the others lost the only thing they had going for them. Then again, a lot of rabbits would be spared. Was that a good thing or a bad thing?

She didn't feel like she slept, but she must have because she suddenly became aware of the sky being light, the crash of dumpsters being emptied in the car park, and the cacophony of birds in the trees outside her window. She rolled onto her side and winced as pain seared through her shoulder and hip. The gash on her shin throbbed fiercely. She'd probably get some horrible raging infection. She examined her legs and found that they were covered in bruises. Nino's bandaging work was impressive, but she didn't have the stomach just then to peel it back and inspect the damage under it.

She got up and put the kettle on to make herself an instant coffee. The message from Gary was on the floor. She picked it up and threw it in the bin. Then she pulled it back out, tore it into four pieces, and threw the pieces in the bin.

When the coffee was made, she stood at the window sipping it and gazing out at the car park, where a hotel worker roamed aimlessly with a leaf blower, sending little eddies of rubbish swirling across the pavement. At the hotel's side entrance, bundles of clean linen were being tossed onto the footpath from the back of a boxy white truck. The early morning sunlight gleamed off the concrete buildings in the industrial park on the other side of the highway.

Erin crossed the room and set her empty coffee cup down beside the phone on the dark wooden table between the two beds. Her briefcase lay on the still-made second bed. She sat down beside it and ran her hand along its smooth leather.

Whether you're a lion or a gazelle – when you wake up, you'd better hit the ground running.

*Like it or not, you're a lion. So be a fucking lion.*

She picked up the phone and dialled reception. 'Good morning,' she said. 'I need the number for the sheriff's office, please.'

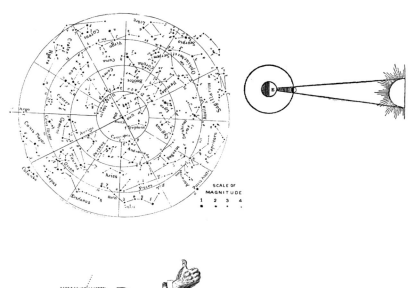

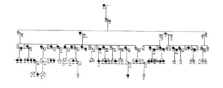

# ACKNOWLEDGEMENTS

**OH, HELLO!** If you are reading this, you must be like me: I always read the acknowledgements at the end of a book. I'm not sure why, since it's mostly just a list of names that mean nothing to me. I guess I enjoy the behind-the-scenes glimpse you get of the author and all the people who supported them in the book's creation. But I think it's also a reluctance to leave. If it's a book I really enjoyed, I'm sad when I reach the end; reading the acknowledgements is a way of lingering a little while longer in its world.

Now I get to write an acknowledgements section of my very own! I hope that you will find it satisfactory.

So. First and foremost, my tremendous gratitude goes to Bronwyn Mehan, CEO of the Spineless Wonders publishing empire, true champion of Australian literature, and bringer-together of all sorts of amazing people. Thanks as well to Linda Godfrey and the rest of the Spineless Wonders team.

Also a great big thanks goes to my editor, the ingenious and eagle-eyed Dr Josh Mei-Ling Dubrau, for all her input and suggestions. I can't imagine a better person to have been paired up with.

And a gigantic thanks also goes to the designer and illustrator of this volume, the venerable Dr Zoë Sadokierski, one of the best book designers on the planet and an eminent academic on the subject of book design and publishing.

I wish to thank the members of my writers group, 'The Beak', which was founded ten years ago in a hazy pub after a UTS writing class and stills meets every couple of months. I pay my respects to Beak members past and present, but particularly to the stalwarts: the aforementioned Zoë S., Lynne Blundell and Richard Waters. If you liked the stories in this book – well, those three had a lot to do with them.

I send general thanks to the writing program at UTS (that's the University of Technology, Sydney, if you don't know), and particular thanks to lecturers Margot Nash and Tegan Bennett Daylight.

Thanks to Julie Shapiro for turning 'Poioumenon' into an awesome radio piece, and to Reuben Field for turning 'Robber' and 'Gecko' into awesome short films.

Thanks also to my parents, Bruce and Ruth Steiner, for always supporting my creative pursuits in general and writing in particular.

I am grateful for various reasons to the following people: Helen Meany, Dave Orwell, Kat di Rocco, Jenn Tench, Andy Robbins, Neil Cronin, Dilini Perera, Thomas Esslinger, and Caitlin Hickie.

And then there is the most important one: thank you to my wife, Bettina Kaiser, who not only gave me excellent feedback on many of these stories, but also has a deep respect for all creative endeavours and made sure I had the time and space I needed to get this book done. Without her support and encouragement, you would not be holding this book.

Well, that's the end of the acknowledgements, and so the end of the book, for real. It's over. Thank you for reading it. Now close it, put it down, and go back to real life. Make yourself some toast, maybe.

# NOTES

Some stories in this book have been published, broadcast or adapted into short films, sometimes in slightly different versions, as follows:

'Turtles' was published in *What You Do and Don't Want: 2007 UTS Writers Anthology*, ABC Books (2007)

'Robber' and 'Gecko' were published in *We All Need a Witness: 2008 UTS Writers Anthology*, Brandl & Schlesinger (2008)

'Poioumenon' was published in *Escape: An Anthology of Short Stories*, Spineless Wonders (2011)

'Tooth' and 'How to Install' were published in *Flashing the Square: Microfiction & Prose Poems*, Spineless Wonders (2014)

'Robber' and 'Gecko' were both adapted into short films by director Reuben Field (2014/2015)

'Poioumenon' was adapted into a radio piece for ABC Radio National Creative Audio Unit's program *Radiotonic* by producer Julie Shapiro (2015)

SPINELESS WONDERS
www.shortaustralianstories.com.au

CPSIA information can be obtained
at www.ICGtesting.com
Printed in the USA
FFOW04n0352110816
26572FF